Too Many Holidays?

Too Many Holidays?

Angela Shelf Medearis
Illustrated by Robert Papp

AN
APPLE
PAPERBACK

New York   Toronto   London   Auckland   Sydney
Mexico City   New Delhi   Hong Kong   Buenos Aires

ISBN 0-439-52327-3

Text copyright © 2003 by Angela Shelf Medearis.
Illustrations copyright © 2003 by Scholastic Inc.

12 11 10 9 8 7 6 5   6 7 8/0
                                                          40

Printed in the U.S.A.
First printing, December 2003

*To my favorite 4th grade class, led by super teacher,
Ms. Susan Bailes, and for my girls Anysa Medearis Bailey,
Caitlin Mullen, Kaleigh Norris, and Karly Harper.
Thanks for making my grandbaby's 4th grade
experience so much fun!*
—Angela Shelf Medearis

Contents

Contents

Chapter One

The Holiday Project

My day began with a nightmare. Ms. Susan Bailes, my fifth-grade teacher, stood in front of the class, smiling. This is usually a good sign. She's a great teacher. So far, she's made my move from my old school in Wichita, Kansas, and my late arrival at Casey Elementary School smoother than I had expected. I was on the edge of really enjoying myself in Austin, Texas, until this morning.

"Okay, everyone, I have a big surprise for you," Ms. Bailes said.

I sat up along with the rest of the class. We waited anxiously for the good news. Were we having a party this Friday? Sometimes, if we'd been really good, Ms. Bailes brought treats to class.

Then I thought about everything that had happened this past week. I slumped down in my chair. As I recall, we hadn't been that good. I, for one, had opened the ferret's cage, sort of by accident. I say "sort of" because I was trying to see if Jerret the Ferret would do a trick for me. But instead of doing a flip, he raced out of the cage. I tried to grab him, but he ran past me. I chased after him, but I tripped over a chair. I tried to break my fall by grabbing Caitlin Mullen's arm. She tipped out of her chair and landed on the floor, and I fell across her legs. Then Ms. Bailes ran over to help us and stumbled over my outstretched leg. When her knee hit the floor, I knew she was really hurt by the look on her face. She twisted her knee, and now she has to wear a brace. Caitlin wasn't hurt, but we both feel terrible about what happened to Ms. Bailes.

In light of everything that went on, I don't think Ms. Bailes is feeling up to a party on Friday. I didn't have to wonder for long what she was so excited about.

"Class, I have decided that we're going to do something different for the holidays this year," Ms. Bailes said. "For a social studies project, I want you to write about how the holidays are celebrated all over the world. We're going to team up and do reports. They'll be due when we return to school on January sixth. Today is Monday, so that gives you four days before our school break begins to come up with your topics. Isn't that exciting?"

We were stunned. Why on earth did she think having a homework assignment over the winter break would make us happy? I wanted to say something, but I was trying my best not to bring attention to myself. The last thing I wanted to do was open my big mouth and get myself into trouble.

Phyllis Muhammad raised her hand. "Ms. Bailes," she said, "my family doesn't celebrate Christmas."

"That's fine, Phyllis," Ms. Bailes said. "You might want to explore what your family does during the holiday season, or you can study another culture. Now, come on, take those frowns off your faces and team up. We'll have teams of two. That way, it will make it easier for you to agree on something. Okay, everyone! Pick a partner."

We looked around at one another. No one wanted to be the first one to move.

"I could always assign partners myself," Ms. Bailes said.

That threat got us moving. I looked around. This was a no-brainer. I walked over to Hannah Lowenstein's desk. She's my best friend. I didn't have to rush — Hannah isn't very popular. I'm her only friend. When I first moved here, Hannah was my only friend, too.

Then, shortly after I arrived, Hannah and I started a drama club. I wrote a play called *The Outside Girl*. I was the director and in charge of choosing people for the parts. Everyone wanted to be in the play, so I became popular overnight. We were in the newspapers and everything. For some reason, once the play was over, Hannah's popularity died. As for me, I was still okay as far as the class was concerned.

I don't know why Hannah is still an outcast in

our fifth-grade class. Maybe it's because she dresses really strange and she has a huge cloud of red hair that she never seems to comb. I like her, and I've gotten used to the way she is. Working on a project with Hannah would be fun.

Ms. Bailes surveyed the room. I could see crinkles forming around her eyes, which was not a good sign. I followed her gaze. But I didn't see the problem she was seeing. Now she was outright frowning.

"You know what, folks," Ms. Bailes said. "I'm a little disappointed. I'd hoped I wouldn't have to do this again."

I had no clue what she was talking about. I knew that we wouldn't have to wait long to find out what she meant.

"You have partnered with the same people I see you with every single day of the year," Ms. Bailes said with a frown. "The holiday season means something, folks. It means we should open our hearts. A new year is beginning, which means fresh starts. So, let me see . . ."

Ms. Bailes looked around the room. I tried to disappear, but it didn't work.

"Hannah Lowenstein," Ms. Bailes said, "you go over there with Anysa Bailey. Karly Norris can partner with Phyllis Muhammad."

Karly raised her hand. "But, Ms. Bailes, she just said her family doesn't celebrate Christmas."

"Okay," Ms. Bailes said, "but maybe they celebrate the new year, or you and Phyllis can pick another culture to study. Either way, she's your partner. And you . . ."

I squeezed my eyes closed. *Please don't let me be the person Ms. Bailes is talking to,* I thought to myself. I was hoping that if I didn't look at her, she would forget I was there.

"Caitlin Mullen," Ms. Bailes said, "go partner with Sharie Johnson."

I blinked. Did she say me?

"Who did you say my partner was, Ms. Bailes?" I asked.

Half the class yelled in unison, "Caitlin Mullen!"

"Caitlin, please go to Sharie's desk. Now, let's move on, class."

Caitlin trudged over to my desk. "I can't believe this! Homework over the holidays!" she mumbled.

"I can't believe it, either," I whispered back. Caitlin and I let out huge sighs. Then we giggled. We love acting, and we're both drama queens.

Ms. Bailes ignored us. "Please turn your desks so that you're facing your partner. Then work on choosing a topic."

Caitlin and I just stared at each other. We couldn't believe we'd have to work during the holidays. It just didn't seem fair.

I rummaged around in my desk until I found my black marker. I marked a big X through Ms. Bailes's name on the front of my notebook where it said FAVORITE TEACHER. I held up the notebook, pretending to read, so she could see the cover. Caitlin saw my notebook and covered her hand with her mouth to keep from laughing. Ms. Bailes cleared her throat and raised an eyebrow.

I sighed and looked at Caitlin. She rolled her eyes and pulled some paper out of her notebook. I grabbed a pen and some paper, too.

"Let's just do this report and get it over with," Caitlin said. "I can't believe we're going to have homework during the holidays. I'm going to be busy celebrating! My father's family is coming from Greece to visit us for Christmas. Wait! That's it! We can do a project about how the Greeks celebrate Christmas. We can write about my family's holiday celebration."

"Well," I said, "I want to do a project about how my family celebrates Christmas. We always have a lot of fun."

"Well, my family's celebration is really going to be unusual and special," she said. "I don't know anyone else who will be celebrating Christmas in the Greek tradition."

"I think we're supposed to agree on a topic," I said stubbornly.

"Well," Caitlin said, "I don't want to do a report on how your family celebrates Christmas."

As much as I hated the fact that Caitlin always

seemed to get her way, I decided that I'd be better off if I just went along with her.

"Okay," I said. "We'll do a report on how your family celebrates a Greek Christmas."

"Great!" Caitlin said, smiling. "My family is going to have fun! We're going to do all the things my father used to do when he was a little boy in Greece. You'll love it! Just you wait and see!"

I had a bad feeling about working with Caitlin. Somehow whenever we worked together on a project, something went wrong.

Chapter Two

Good News?

By the time I got home, I had a headache. I put my head down on the kitchen table.

"What's wrong, Sharie?" Momma asked. "I haven't seen you this way in a long time."

"Yeah," Sandra said. "You look even worse than usual. Momma, can't you make her dress any neater?"

"It's not my fault that my every waking thought is not about clothes, Miss Fashion Queen," I said grumpily.

"Both of you stop it," Momma said. "Sharie, did you have a bad day at school?"

"Momma, that girl always has a bad day. Just look at how she's dressed," Sandra said.

"Momma, make her leave me alone."

"Sandra, stop it," Momma said.

I told Momma about my assignment.

"Well, that seems like a wonderful assignment," Momma said.

"I knew you'd be on Ms. Bailes's side," I said, frowning.

"I'm not on her side, Sharie," Momma said. "I just think the world would be a better place if we worked together and tried to understand one another."

"Yeah, well, I don't want to do homework during the holidays," I said. "And besides, Caitlin Mullen is my partner, and she wants to study a Greek Christmas celebration."

"Isn't she the girl who you fell on?" Sandra asked.

I couldn't believe Sandra was telling on me. Sandra is best friends with Karly Norris's big sister, Jennie. Karly tells Jennie everything I do in school. Then Jennie tells Sandra. It's not fair! I don't tell Sandra everything Karly does at school. I guess it's because Karly never does anything to get into trouble.

"You fell on Caitlin?" Momma asked. "How on earth did that happen?"

"I didn't mean to. That was a week ago. It was an accident." I told Momma about Jerret the Ferret and everything that had happened, including the part about Ms. Bailes hurting her leg.

"Hmm. Well, I think it was very wise for Ms. Bailes to put you two together," Momma said. "Go on and lay down until dinner, Sharie. Your daddy will be home in a little while. We've got some news to tell you that might make you feel better."

"What is it?" I asked.

"Just wait," Momma said. "Don't be so impatient. We'll tell you at dinner tonight."

"Okay," I said as I dragged myself upstairs.

I lay across the bed, but I couldn't sleep. I was too worried about school. My grades and my attitude were pretty bad when I first moved to Texas. I didn't want to go to a new school, and I didn't do my homework. My grades started to slip, but I improved my work habits and everything changed for the better.

Momma and Daddy are so proud that I've brought up my grades. Now it isn't only Sandra being complimented on her schoolwork. My parents promised that if I keep getting good marks, I could go to theater camp this summer. Ms. Bailes works there as a camp counselor. You get to write a play with your group and put it on. Ms. Bailes said that we even get to take trips to watch professional plays. I can't wait until theater camp starts! I won't let anything mess up my grades.

I rolled over and rubbed my eyes. My head was still pounding, but I couldn't stop thinking about our homework assignment. I needed an A in social studies. The only way to get an A was to make sure the project that Caitlin and I turned in was really, really good.

That night, dinner started out great. Daddy brought home some of Austin's famous barbecued ribs. I love them more than Sandra does, so that means Daddy was thinking about me when he bought them. We were eating our dessert when Daddy said, "Your momma has some news for you."

If you moved into our house, it would take a while to hear my mother's and father's names. Daddy always said, "your momma," and Momma always said, "your daddy." Actually, sometimes Momma did say, "Howard," but Daddy never said, "Angeline," unless he was doing business on the telephone and he had to tell someone Momma's name. That's just one of the many weird things about my family.

I can always tell when Momma is excited about something. She smiles from ear to ear and sits up real straight in her chair.

Sandra and I sat up straight, too. Sandra winked at me. I winked back. Daddy would say something if he noticed either of us slumped at the table. Daddy has perfect navy posture, and he wants us to stand tall, too. To avoid hearing him lecture, we try to remind each other to sit up straight.

"Why don't you tell them," Momma said to Daddy.

I glanced at Sandra and rolled my eyes. She started to giggle and ate a spoonful of chocolate pudding to cover it up. If Daddy has some news to tell, it usually isn't what I want to hear. He's always think-ing up household projects that require scrubbing, dusting, or sweeping. Momma said this is what he did in the navy. Now that he's out of the navy, he sees us as his shipmates or his deckhands. I'll be glad when he realizes that he's out of the navy now and that we're his daughters.

"It's your idea, honey. You tell them," Daddy said.

"Will someone please just say it," I blurted out.

Sandra laughed at me, but she wanted to know what was going on as much as I did. Her strategy was to stay on my parents' good side by keeping quiet. My strategy usually was to open my big mouth and then get into trouble.

"Okay, I'll tell you," Momma said. "We've decided that this year, in honor of our first new home and the new baby, we're going to celebrate Kwanzaa."

"That's great, Momma," Sandra said, like she'd just been told she was getting everything she wanted for Christmas for the rest of her life.

"What does that mean?" I asked. "What about Christmas?"

"Don't get all worried, honey," Daddy said. "We'll decorate for Christmas, too."

"Yes," said Momma. "And in the spirit of Kwanzaa, we're going to exchange handmade gifts."

I could see the look of horror on Sandra's face. She showed me her Christmas list last week. One thing is for sure, I've never heard of a handmade karaoke machine. I waited for Sandra to say something. But as usual, she kept her cool. She didn't even flinch. I wish I could have done the same, but I couldn't keep my mouth shut. Not me.

"That isn't fair," I said loudly.

"Sharie, please don't spoil this for your momma," Daddy said. "This is what she wants to do. It's good to start new traditions in a family when you're going to have a new baby."

"I don't want to celebrate Kwanzaa *or* make presents! Can't we just wait until next year when the baby is here? Wouldn't that be better?"

"This isn't just about the baby," Momma said. "It's about teaching both of you about our culture. Kwanzaa isn't a religious holiday, it's a cultural one."

"I think it's a great idea," Sandra said.

"Oh, give me a break, Sandra!" I said.

"Okay, here's the deal," Daddy said. "Kwanzaa will be part of our holiday celebration this year. We're making gifts like your momma wants, and that's that."

Daddy picked up his fork and started eating his dinner again. In my house, that means the discussion is over. If Momma wants to do something and Daddy backs her up, not even a visit from Santa Claus himself would change their minds.

"May I go to my room, please?" I asked. I wanted to get out of there. Nothing was going well for me today.

"No. Finish your dessert first," Daddy said.

I stirred my chocolate pudding around and around, but I didn't feel like eating any more of it. That's when I knew I was really upset. I love chocolate. I don't think Daddy has ever had to tell me to finish eating my dessert before.

"I thought you'd be excited about this, Sharie,"

Momma said. "Just think, maybe you and that girl in your class . . . what's her name?"

"Caitlin," Sandra said.

"Yes, Caitlin," Momma continued. "Maybe you and Caitlin can do a project about our Kwanzaa celebration."

I wondered for the thousandth time if Momma was from another planet.

"Are you kidding?" I said. "She's not going to want to do a project on a Black holiday, Momma."

"Now, wait a minute," Daddy said. "Kwanzaa isn't just for African Americans. I know white families who have participated in Kwanzaa celebrations."

I stared at Daddy. He must be Mr. Outer Space.

"Where did that happen, Daddy? You mean, families in the navy?"

"Well, yes."

"That's just what I thought," I said.

"Our Kwanzaa is open to anyone who wants to join us for a celebration," Daddy said. "Feel free to invite Caitlin if you want to. I'm sure she'll enjoy it."

Daddy doesn't seem to realize that our new school and the kids in Austin are totally different from what we were used to on navy bases.

"That's just it, Daddy," I said. "Casey Elementary isn't like the navy. There are only four Black kids in my entire school, including me."

"So maybe you and Caitlin can teach your class something when you do your report about Kwanzaa," Daddy said.

"Exactly," Momma said.

"Right," I said. "But Caitlin is determined to do a project about how the Greeks celebrate Christmas, not what our family plans to do."

"Just what is that supposed to mean?" Daddy asked.

"Nothing," I said. "It means nothing. Now may I be excused?"

"Yes, go on. Sometimes I just don't know what's wrong with you," Daddy said. "I thought you'd like to celebrate Kwanzaa."

I looked at Daddy. He was serious. He really thought I'd rather have some silly handmade gift instead of a cool computer game from the Computer Wizard store.

"Good night," I said. It was no use trying to explain anything to Daddy. He just didn't understand about all the changes I'd been through, about my social studies project, or about how much I wanted the things on my Christmas list. I ran into my room, shut the door, and dived onto my bed.

Chapter Three

Too Many Holidays?

"Sharie," Sandra said, banging on my door. "Momma said it's your night to do the dishes."

"Go away, Miss I-don't-want-Christmas," I shouted.

Sandra opened the door. She put her hands on her hips and just looked at me. I pulled the pillow over my head.

"Hey, I can't wait to make your Kwanzaa present," Sandra said sweetly. "I'll probably make you a mask out of a paper bag so I'll have something pretty to look at for a change."

"Go away," I said. "Leave me alone!"

"Okay, but look," Sandra said. "If Mom and Dad

want to try something new, just go along with it. It's no big deal. You know they change their minds all the time. Come on! Cheer up and get downstairs before you get into trouble."

"Maybe this new plan for the holidays isn't a big deal to you," I said, "but it is to me."

"Okay, suit yourself," Sandra said. "But you better get down there and wash those dishes before Daddy goes in the kitchen."

I rolled over and pulled the pillow tighter around my head. I didn't want to make any stupid presents. I was never any good in arts and crafts. In second grade, I was asked to skip my turn decorating the bulletin board. That's how bad I was. I mean, once I tried to draw a bunny and everyone, including Momma, thought it was a frog. Sandra could draw practically anything. I shook my head. It just wasn't fair: a new school, a new baby, and a new holiday — all in one year.

The phone rang. I heard Momma calling me. I went down to the kitchen. Hannah usually called me around the same time every night. I decided that I might as well clean the dishes while I talked on the phone. I picked up the receiver.

"Hello?"

I was right. It was Hannah.

"Hey, did you decide on your project with Caitlin yet?"

"I guess so," I said as I rinsed a handful of silverware. "What about you and Anysa?"

"Yes! We've got a great plan! She's really nice!" Hannah said. "I've never really had a chance to talk to her before. She's always hanging out with Caitlin."

"What did you two decide to do for your project?"

"Actually, that's why I'm calling you," Hannah said. "We're doing our report on Hanukkah. I wanted to know if you'd like to come over and celebrate the first night of Hanukkah with us. I'd feel bad if Anysa came and my best friend wasn't even invited."

I didn't even know what Hanukkah was except that it's a Jewish holiday. I was pretty sure it was boring.

"It's okay if I don't come over. I know you're doing it for school," I said as I rinsed a plate and put it into the dishwasher. "Just go ahead and invite Anysa."

"But I want you to come, too," Hannah said, almost whining. "Please."

"I have to ask my parents," I said. For the first time, I hoped they'd say no. Being forced to celebrate Kwanzaa was bad enough.

"I'll wait," Hannah said.

"What? Well, let's see if Anysa is coming first, since she's your partner. Then I'll ask my parents if I can come."

"It doesn't matter. I want you to come either way."

My only way out now was my parents. I would have to carefully word the way I asked them about Hanukkah. I wanted to make it sound like going would be a problem so that they would say no.

"I'll ask them later," I said. "They're busy right now. I'll tell you tomorrow at school."

"Promise me you'll ask them, okay? My mom needs to know how many people are coming over."

I hesitated. This was turning out to be an even more horrible day. Nothing was going well for me.

"Promise me!" Hannah said. "A best-friend promise."

Hannah was very serious about our friendship. She'd stuck up for me when no one else would. When I first came to Casey, Hannah was the one who sat with me in the cafeteria when everyone else ignored me. She was also partly the reason I was even slightly popular, since it was her idea, along with mine, to start the drama club.

"Sure," I said finally. "I promise I'll ask them right away. A best-friend promise."

"Cool beans! 'Bye! See you tomorrow!"

"Okay," I said. "'Bye."

Hannah hung up. I sat there holding the receiver in my hand. Oh, brother! Another holiday headache! Why couldn't things just stay the same? I didn't want to try anything new for the holidays. I wished that we could go back to the way things were before: the same decorations, lots of gifts from our wish lists, and a big Christmas dinner. That's all I wanted for Christmas.

Sandra came into the kitchen.

"Momma," Sandra yelled. "This girl is sitting here just holding the phone so I can't use it."

"I am not!" I yelled. "I had a phone call."

"Yeah," Sandra said, "like someone would call you."

"Leave me alone, Sandra."

Momma walked into the kitchen. "Both of you stop it right now! Sharie, let your sister use the phone."

I hung up the phone and followed Momma into the dining room.

"Hannah wants me to ask you something important, Momma."

"Does she want to come over tomorrow?" Momma asked.

Whenever Hannah's mother went out of town, Momma usually let Hannah stay with us.

"No, she wants me to skip Christmas and instead celebrate the first night of Hanukkah with her family."

28

I said it before I could stop myself. I hoped that Momma would be so shocked that she would say no.

"Does her mother know about this?" Momma asked.

"Yes, I'm sure she does," I lied. I was digging myself deeper and deeper into a bigger mess. I couldn't seem to stop myself. "I'll just tell her you said that I can't go."

This was working out perfectly.

"Honey, could you come in here a moment?" Momma called to Daddy.

I frowned. No, no, no. Daddy would want me to go to Hannah's celebration. Then he'd invite her family over for Kwanzaa. He loved for us to have what he likes to call "new cultural experiences."

"It's okay, Momma," I said quickly. "I don't mind not going. Really. You don't have to bother Daddy."

"Yes, ma'am," Daddy said, saluting Momma. "Captain Johnson on duty, ma'am."

Daddy could be so navy corny, it wasn't even funny anymore.

"Hannah invited Sharie over to her house for a

Hanukkah celebration. What do you think about her going?"

"Sure, let her go. She should be exposed to other religions."

"Daddy, it's okay," I said. "I've read about Hanukkah at school."

Sandra clutched her heart like she was shocked. "Sharie can read?"

"Poke your big nose into someone else's business, Sandra," I said.

"Girls!" Momma said. "Honey, Sharie also said something about the first night of Hanukkah being on the same day as Christmas."

"I'm pretty sure that Hanukkah begins before Christmas this year," Daddy said.

I dropped my head. Maybe I went a little overboard. Suppose they asked Mrs. Lowenstein or Hannah about what I said. I would be in trouble. No, more than in trouble. This was getting out of hand. In my short life, I have come to understand one thing for sure: Lying is a never-ending trap.

"I think she should go," Daddy said.

"You're right, honey," Momma said. "It was nice of Hannah to invite Sharie over for Hanukkah. It will be a great learning experience."

"That's right, Sharie," Daddy said. "Your Uncle Fred is a Muslim, and my sister, Carolyn, is a Buddhist. We want to teach you girls to respect everyone's beliefs."

"Okay, Sharie," Momma said. "You can go to Hannah's for the first night of Hanukkah."

I was having one of the worst days of my life. And tomorrow, I would have to admit I could celebrate Hanukkah with Hannah. How did I get myself into this mess?

The next morning, I switched off my alarm and dragged myself out of bed. I climbed into the shower. When I'm feeling really good, I sing in the shower. Other times, I hum. Today, I just leaned my head against the tile and let the water run over me.

I dreaded facing Ms. Bailes. As soon as our social studies class began, she called on each team to describe their project.

31

Anysa and Hannah went first.

"We're going to celebrate our holidays together," Anysa said. "Hannah's coming to my house for Christmas, and I'm going to her house during Hanukkah."

"We're going to write poems about our experiences," Hannah said.

"That sounds wonderful," Ms. Bailes said. "You have an excellent idea. Okay, folks. Anyone else who plans on doing their reports in a way that each person experiences something new gets an extra ten points. Now, I'd like to remind all of you that time is running out to settle on a topic. Okay, let's continue. Next volunteers?"

People were jumping up quicker than popcorn in a microwave to explain their projects. There were only a few teams left. I prayed for the bell to ring. It didn't.

"Excellent," Ms. Bailes said. "Everyone has their projects planned with extra days to spare."

Kermine Woolsey raised his hand and shook it wildly.

"Yes, Kermine," Ms. Bailes said. "Do you have something to add?"

"Everyone hasn't reported on their projects yet."

"Oh, really?" Ms. Bailes said. "Did I miss someone?"

"Two people, one team," Kermine volunteered.

"Which team?" Ms. Bailes asked, shaking her head. "I thought I had everyone. Let me see. Wait, you're right. Hmm." She looked straight at me and then at Caitlin.

"No wonder you girls are so quiet," Ms. Bailes said. "Okay, come on. There's no getting around this. What's your project?"

"Our report will be on the Greeks' celebration of Christmas. My father is part Greek, you know. He's always telling me about when he was a child and his family had a huge celebration at Christmastime. My father has several family members who still live in Greece. This year, for the first time, we plan on bringing my grandmother and some family members from Greece to Austin for Christmas. At least a half dozen or more of them are coming to spend the holidays with us, but as you know, we live in a large house, so we'll have room for everyone."

"What house?" Kermine said. "Give us a break! You mean that huge *mansion* you live in."

Ms. Bailes slowly put the roll book on her desk.

"That comment wasn't necessary, Kermine."

Ms. Bailes looked over at me and then back at Caitlin.

"You do remember that this project has to be a team effort," Ms. Bailes said. "Caitlin, you and Sharie plan to work together on this project, correct?"

It wasn't fair that Caitlin always got her way. I raised my hand.

"Yes, Sharie?"

"I've decided I don't want to do a report on a Greek Christmas. So can I choose someone else to be my partner?" I looked at Caitlin, and she looked hurt.

Ms. Bailes frowned. "First off, everyone has a partner, and they've all managed to figure out what to do. Everyone, that is, except you two. So, even if I were open to that suggestion, which I'm not, it would still end up being just the two of you left. The bottom line is that you have until Friday before our winter break starts to pick a topic. Do you understand me?"

"Yes," I said, "but this is so unfair."

"Whoever told you life was fair was mistaken," Ms. Bailes said. "Now, everyone take out your spelling books and turn to page forty."

Ms. Bailes had her hands on her hips. That meant trouble, but I raised my hand again. I couldn't seem to stop myself.

"What if we each come up with something spectacular all by ourselves, put a lot of hard work and effort into it, and then do it as a report. Will that help?"

"The only thing that will help you is for you and Caitlin to work together. You need to learn how to cooperate. That's part of what this assignment is about. Now, not another word unless you have a question or comment about the present lesson or you're ready to explain your project. Is that clear?"

"Yes," I said quietly.

I knew I had pushed Ms. Bailes too far. She meant business. I was stuck with Caitlin, and that was that.

Ms. Bailes tapped her foot. "Caitlin, what about you? Is that clear?"

"Yes," Caitlin said softly.

Chapter Four

From Bad to Worse!

We were in the cafeteria when my day went from bad to worse. I overheard Caitlin talking about me. I heard her telling Anysa and Karly that I was hard to get along with and as stubborn as a mule. Then she laughed and said, "Come to think of it, Sharie looks like a mule, too."

I was furious. I walked over to where she was sitting and stood over her.

"I heard what you said." I stood next to Caitlin with my fists tightly clenched. She looked up at me.

"Would you move downwind, please? I can't breathe."

Everyone sitting near Caitlin thought what she said was pretty funny. I was so mad that I was starting to get a headache.

"Yeah, well, at least my mother wants to see me more than once a year."

Suddenly, everyone was silent. Caitlin stared at me. She gasped for air like I had hit her really hard in the stomach. Then she ran out of the cafeteria.

"That was really mean," Anysa said as she got up to follow Caitlin.

"She was saying mean things about me!" I said.

"You don't understand," Anysa said. "You should be ashamed."

Me? What about Caitlin? She was just as much at fault. I got my lunch and sat down. I could hear all the kids whispering. When Hannah came into the cafeteria, she sat down with me. She didn't even notice that all the kids were staring at me.

"Aren't you hungry?" Hannah asked.

"No," I said.

"Do you mind if I eat your peaches? I'm starving."

"Go ahead," I said. I felt terrible. My head was throbbing. I felt like I was going to be sick.

Karly walked over. "Nice job, Sharie. Now you'll never get your project done."

"Why don't you leave me alone?" I said.

"Caitlin is always crying about missing her mother. Didn't you know that?" Karly said.

"Know what?" Hannah said. "What is she talking about?"

"That was really mean," Karly said as she walked away.

"What happened?" Hannah asked.

"Caitlin said I look and act like a mule, so I said something mean back to her. Caitlin started crying, and everyone sided with her. She can talk about anyone she wants to, but you'd better not say anything about her or it's a disaster."

"Yeah, tell me about it," Hannah said.

After lunch, Ms. Bailes called me into the hallway. She had her hands on her hips again, which meant I was in big trouble.

"What has gotten into you, Sharie? It's not like you to be in so much trouble. You were doing so much better in school."

"What did I do now?" I asked.

"You hurt Caitlin's feelings. You know that her mother's acting career keeps her away from home for months at a time. You didn't have to bring up the fact that her mother is hardly ever in town."

"She started it. She said I look like a mule. Did you know that?"

Ms. Bailes sighed. "I spoke to Caitlin about the incident. You were both wrong. You need to think before you speak."

"And Caitlin doesn't have to?"

"Yes, Caitlin needs to think, too," Ms. Bailes agreed. "I hope this project will bring the two of you together. I'm counting on both of you to rise to the challenge. I know you can do it."

Ms. Bailes squeezed my shoulder.

"I want you to apologize to each other and agree to work cooperatively on this project," Ms. Bailes said.

"Okay," I said slowly.

"Caitlin, may I see you in the hall?" Ms. Bailes asked. "Class, please continue with your reading assignment. I'll be back in a moment."

Caitlin stood next to me in the hallway. She refused to look at me. I didn't look at her, either.

Ms. Bailes put her hands on her hips again.

"Girls, apologize to each other and promise me that you'll do your very best to work together on your project during the winter break."

I waited for Caitlin to apologize first, since she had started it. When she didn't say anything, I didn't say anything, either. Then I decided I might as well get it over with. I know how stubborn Caitlin can be.

"I'm sorry, Caitlin," I said. "I was upset and I hurt your feelings. I promise I'll cooperate on our project."

There, it was over! Knowing Caitlin, we would be standing there until it was time to graduate from high school before she apologized.

"I'm sorry, too," Caitlin said.

"And . . ." Ms. Bailes said firmly. "I think you owe Sharie a little more than a simple 'I'm sorry.'"

"And I never should have said you look like a mule. That was mean," Caitlin said softly.

"And . . ." Ms. Bailes said.

"And I promise to cooperate with you on our project," Caitlin said quickly.

Suddenly, I felt better. At least Ms. Bailes was fair. Everyone else treats Caitlin like she's the queen of the fifth grade. Caitlin was the I-can-do-no-wrong girl. She was always the I'm-too-beautiful-to-mess-up princess. And me, I was just plain-old-always-in-trouble Sharie Johnson.

As soon as I got home, I took a nap. Sometimes sleeping helps when I have a headache. This time it didn't. I had too much on my mind. If I didn't figure out how to work with Caitlin and get a good grade on this project, I would be in trouble with Momma and Daddy, too. Nothing was worth that.

I fell back on my last resort — talking to Sandra. I had to be desperate to talk to my big sister about my problems. Even though she's only two years older than me, she thinks she's my momma. She's always telling me what to do, and she always has something smart to say. Plus, she's always complaining about me. The worst thing is that she's usually right. That's what gets me!

Sandra is smart and talented, and she can play the piano like a junior Mozart. When it comes to looks, whenever someone meets the two of us together, they spend fifteen minutes telling Momma how beautiful Sandra is. Then they say something like, "Oh, is this your daughter, too? Uh, she's cute."

"Sandra," I called, tapping on her door. "Can I come in for a minute? I need to talk to you."

"What do you want?" Sandra asked. "Go away, I'm reading."

I bit my bottom lip to avoid making a smart remark.

"It'll take just a minute," I said.

"Can you make it quick?" Sandra asked.

I rolled my eyes and sighed one of Ms. Bailes's long sighs. "Yes! Come on, Sandra. I need some help." I couldn't believe I was begging Sandra for help.

"Please," I said softly. If Momma heard me trying to talk with Sandra, she would know something was seriously wrong and question me about it.

"Okay, but only for a minute," Sandra said.

"Can I sit on your chair?" I asked. You had to ask permission to do anything — including breathing, almost — in Sandra's room. She was a neat freak, just like Daddy. She didn't want anyone touching anything or crinkling up her bedcovers. Unlike my junky room, everything was neatly in place in her room.

"Yes, but don't touch anything on my dresser," she warned.

I sat with my hands folded on my lap. I explained the social studies project and about how much I needed a good grade. I told her that Caitlin was making fun of me. I told her about what I said to Caitlin and our promise to Ms. Bailes that we'd try to get along and work on our project together. I told her that I only had one more day to figure out a project that Caitlin and I could agree on.

Sandra was still reading her book.

"Are you listening to me?" I asked.

"Unlike you, I can do two things at once," Sandra said.

I bit my lip again, harder this time. This girl was getting on my nerves.

"I don't know what to do," I said. "I want to get a good grade, but I don't think Caitlin wants to work with me anymore."

Sandra put her bookmark inside her book and closed it. I never use a bookmark. I just fold down the corner of the page. Why is Sandra so perfect?

"Do you remember when I had a problem with Carolyn Tate a few years ago?" Sandra said. "I mean, it seemed like we were always arguing."

"Yes, I remember. It's the only time you've ever gotten in trouble at school."

"And do you know how I stopped it?"

"No, not really."

"I did everything I could to get along with her."

"What do you think I should do?"

"If I were you, I would apologize to Caitlin about not wanting to do the report about her family," Sandra said. "Go ahead and do the project that she wants to do and get it over with. You need to get a good grade to go to camp this summer. Like Daddy always says, 'Just go along to get along with her.'"

If Daddy heard her saying that, he'd be so proud that he'd give Sandra a medal. He loves it when we use his little sayings.

"Do you think I should call her on the telephone?"

"Duh, unless you've got psychic powers, how else would you talk to her?"

"Well, I could just talk to her tomorrow," I said.

Sandra really gets on my nerves sometimes, but I had to admit that she was right. I needed to quit being so stubborn about this homework project. I got up to leave.

"You're not even going to thank me?" she said.

"Yes, just give me a minute, will you? Thank you," I said.

I checked the clock. It was only 7:00. It wasn't too late. I could still call Caitlin. I picked up the receiver. Then I quickly put it back down. I walked into my room. I'd better practice what I was going to say first.

I stood in front of the mirror trying to figure out the best words. I stumbled again and again. Finally, I looked at my last social studies paper. It was a C-. Not a C+, not a B, not an A, but a C-. I could average out what my social studies grade was going to be without doing any math calculations. I needed an A on this project. I picked up the telephone and dialed Caitlin's number.

Chapter Five

Naughty or Nice?

"Hello, Mullen residence," Caitlin said.

I stammered, "Hello, is this Caitlin?"

"Yes, this is Caitlin. Who is this?"

She knew who it was.

"It's Sharie," I said.

"Sharie? Sharie who?"

I wanted to slam down the phone. "Sharie Johnson."

"Oh, what do you want?" she said. "And why didn't you call me on my private line?"

I knew that she was just showing off. She knew how much I wanted my own telephone number because I'd foolishly told her.

"I forgot the number," I said.

That wasn't a lie. I had purposely blanked out the fact that every girl in my class had their own phone except for me. Even Hannah had her own telephone. Most of them even had their own cell phones. I wouldn't even dream of asking Daddy for a cell phone. That lecture might continue until I was old enough to get a job and pay for my own phone.

"I called to apologize again," I said finally. "It seems we've gotten off to a bad start on this project. I've already apologized for falling on you and talking about your mother. Now I'm calling to see if we can just move on and get to work on our project."

"I don't recall you apologizing for falling on me," Caitlin said. "I think what you said that day was, 'Ms. Bailes, I had to grab Caitlin to keep from hurting myself.'"

Well, maybe she was right. I didn't exactly apologize that day. I just thought I had.

"I'm sorry," I said. "Really, I am. I didn't do it on purpose."

"What about my book that you ruined? All you

said was, 'Gosh, I didn't realize I was making a mess. Look, you can still read the page even though there's some chocolate on it.'"

"I didn't apologize then, either?" I asked.

Now I was beginning to see why she might still be upset with me. I was always so busy defending myself that I'd forgotten to say I was truly sorry.

"I'm sorry for everything I've done to you. Really, I am," I said. "So can we get started on the project tomorrow?"

"Sure," Caitlin said. "I'll bring the information I have to school. Then we can tell Ms. Bailes that we're doing a report about my Greek family's Christmas celebration."

I grimaced. "No, we're not. I didn't say that. We have to talk about it first. Then we need to agree on something. That's how it's supposed to be — not you just deciding all by yourself what we're going to do."

"I don't understand. Do you already have a project researched?"

"No, not yet." I had been so busy being mad that

I hadn't even thought about it. "I'll have something tomorrow."

"Tomorrow is the last day. I already started working on this. Why can't we just do a Greek Christmas?"

"Because you cannot always have your way."

"What are you talking about? I don't always have my way. This is stupid. You called me, remember? You're the one who doesn't have a project in mind. I already started on one. What is wrong with you learning about a Greek Christmas?"

"First off, my family will celebrate Kwanzaa this year. Besides, I know a lot about the Greek Christmas already."

"Yeah, like what?" she said.

"Don't you worry about it," I said. "I know as much about a Greek Christmas as you know about Kwanzaa."

"I don't think so. I know that Kwanzaa has seven principles. I also know it was invented by a man named Ron Karen."

"Dr. Karenga," I said.

51

"What?"

"His name is Dr. Ron Karenga," I said. I didn't know much, but I knew that. "I'll bet you don't know what the seven principles are."

"You probably don't know them, either," Caitlin said. "Look, this is stupid. I'm hanging up."

"You started it," I said. "I'm hanging up, too. And by tomorrow, I'll have something, you'll see."

"I don't care what you do," Caitlin said, "because I'm doing a Greek Christmas."

"I'll see about that," I said, slamming down the phone. She made me so mad sometimes. I stormed into my room and opened my social studies book, but I was so angry I couldn't concentrate.

I turned on my Game Boy and began to play. Sometimes it relaxed me. Why did I let her get to me like that? She was worse than Sandra.

Later, I looked up Kwanzaa on the Internet. I still didn't want our family to celebrate it, but I wanted to make sure I could tell Caitlin all about it tomorrow. I read about Kwanzaa. I didn't know that the holiday had been celebrated for more than thirty years. There was more to the celebration than just making gifts. I put my head down on my desk. Tomorrow, I would just tell Ms. Bailes that I had everything under control. Of course, I didn't have anything under control. But maybe by the end of the week I could figure something out.

This problem is all snooty Caitlin's fault. She should have just compromised. No one wants to hear all about her old Greek Christmas. I know I don't.

I put on my pajamas and fell onto my bed. I closed my eyes and tried to imagine myself in a department store. I could buy all the wonderful gifts on my Christmas list. I drifted to sleep and dreamed of Santa Claus actually sticking under the tree everything that was on my list. He was about to take a bite from the cookies I'd left for him when Sandra stopped him.

"Sharie's been so naughty. You shouldn't leave her anything."

Santa looked at me sadly and turned to go.

"Oh, Santa," Sandra said sweetly, "I think you're forgetting something."

Sandra pointed at my pile of presents. Santa began to throw my gifts back into his bag.

"Santa, no!" I shouted. "You can't do this to me."

"See, she's rude! She's always trying to tell people what they can and cannot do. I'm not like that, Santa."

He smiled at Sandra. "I know," Santa said. "You're the most perfect girl I've ever known. You're even more perfect than my special Caitlin. It's the two of you who make Christmas so special."

I wanted to bite my tongue, but even in the dream I couldn't keep my big mouth shut. I yelled to him as he stuffed himself up the chimney, "Caitlin and Sandra aren't as sweet as you think!"

I woke up in a sweat. The clock said 6:00 A.M. I would have to get dressed for school in a few minutes. I stared at the ceiling. What on earth would make me get smart with Santa Claus? I had to learn to keep my mouth shut! I couldn't stop talking, even in my dreams.

It was the last day of school before winter break. Ms. Bailes was still excited about the holiday projects.

When it was time for us to work with our partners, Caitlin and I sat silently facing each other.

Ms. Bailes stared down at us. She shook her head. "You two are so much alike, it's not even funny," she said.

I watched her limp back to the front of the room. She didn't even glance at us for the rest of the hour.

I realized this was it. If Caitlin and I left school, there was a good chance we wouldn't have the opportunity to talk during the holidays. Suppose her family went out of town or something? I had never considered that.

At the end of the day, Ms. Bailes gave us all little gifts and wished us a happy holiday. I picked up my backpack and looked around for Caitlin. I saw her standing at her locker.

I decided to tell her how silly I thought we were being and that we'd better figure out how to work together. Suddenly, my mouth was dry. I reached into my backpack for my juice box.

I pulled the straw from the side, peeled off the

plastic wrap, and stuck it in the top of the box. I punched down too hard and juice spurted out everywhere. I looked down at my white blouse. A huge strawberry-colored stain was spreading across the front. Momma would not be happy. She had just bought me this blouse. I tried to tell her I didn't like wearing white. I have a hard time keeping my clothes clean.

I balanced my backpack on my knee and grabbed a Kleenex. I tried scrubbing the stain with the tissue. Then I noticed Caitlin walking toward me. I quickly opened another juice box. I would offer it to her and try to get her to work with me.

"Caitlin, I've got something for you."

I must have been squeezing the sides of the juice box too hard. A stream of juice sprang up into the air and landed on Caitlin's cream-colored sweater. Her face turned as red as the stain. Just then, Ms. Bailes came toward us.

Chapter Six

Going Along to Get Along

"Did I just see what I think I saw?" Ms. Bailes asked.

I squeezed my eyes shut. I wanted to say, "No you didn't."

"I didn't mean to make such a mess. Honest. I was just offering Caitlin some juice."

"Is that true, Caitlin?" Ms. Bailes asked.

Caitlin looked at her sweater and gave me one of the meanest looks I've ever seen. Even when I wasn't looking at her, I could feel her eyes burning into me.

"No," Caitlin said angrily. "She said, 'Caitlin, I've got something for you,' and then sprayed me with that juice."

"Both of you come with me," Ms. Bailes said. "I cannot believe you sometimes, Sharie."

"What?" I said. "I wasn't trying to hurt her. I was offering her some juice."

"I'm sorry, but you will have to answer for this. We're going to the vice-principal's office right now," Ms. Bailes said.

I gathered my things and followed Ms. Bailes and Caitlin. How did this happen? Caitlin walked on the other side of Ms. Bailes, sniffing and wiping away her tears. I'm sure that was to ensure I got into more trouble.

Mr. Applegate took one look at us and cleared his throat. This is always a bad sign. Caitlin told her side first. Then they all looked at me. I explained what happened, including my good intentions when I first opened the juice.

I explained how I wanted to make up with Caitlin and work with her on our project because I needed to get a good grade.

"I think Sharie's telling the truth," Ms. Bailes said. I wanted to say, "Finally someone believes my side of the story," but for a change, I didn't say anything.

"Now that Sharie has explained everything, I suppose it could have happened like that," Mr. Applegate said.

"I'm sorry about everything that has happened," I said. "I really didn't mean to mess up Caitlin's sweater, honest."

I felt bad seeing Caitlin covered with strawberry juice. I was sure the sticky mess wouldn't come out of her cream-colored sweater easily. I thought about what Sandra had said about making friends.

"I know it doesn't seem like it," I said, "but I really like Caitlin."

"Sure you do," Caitlin said through a huge sniffle.

Caitlin reached inside her sleeve to get her handkerchief. She pulled it out and just looked at it. It was covered with strawberry juice, just like her sweater. Caitlin and I looked at each other. She started to giggle. I smiled at her.

Mr. Applegate cleared his throat again and pushed a box of tissues toward Caitlin.

"I want to be friends," I said, smiling at Caitlin. "I keep trying, but I always seem to do the wrong thing."

Caitlin looked surprised. "Really? You really want to be friends?"

"Yes," I said. "I really want to be friends. I'm sorry about everything, okay?"

"Okay," Caitlin said softly. "I'm sorry, too."

"This is all just a misunderstanding and bad timing," Ms. Bailes said.

"Is this problem all over between the two of you?" Mr. Applegate asked. "Can I trust you girls to get along from now on?"

"Yes, sir," I said.

Caitlin nodded her head.

"What about your project?" Ms. Bailes said. "Are you going to work together?"

Ms. Bailes never misses an opportunity to teach a lesson. That's why she's such a good teacher.

"I will if she will," Caitlin said.

"I need a good grade, and I really want to be friends with Caitlin," I said. "I know we can work together during the holidays."

"I know you can come up with a great project to-gether, right?" Ms. Bailes said.

I looked at Caitlin and she looked at me.

"I think we can," I said.

"Yes, we can," Caitlin said. "I've already started the project about my family's Greek Christmas cele-bration, so we can both work on it to finish it. Will you come to my house for a meeting?"

Caitlin was getting her way, as usual.

I sighed heavily. Why didn't I say something first? "Oh, okay," I said.

"You don't sound very enthusiastic," Mr. Apple-gate said. "Ms. Bailes tells me you two have had a problem agreeing on a topic for your project."

"We're enthusiastic. Aren't we, Sharie?" Caitlin said.

"Sure, sure we are," I said. And it was true; I was enthusiastic about getting along with Caitlin and get-ting a good grade on this project.

"Great!" Mr. Applegate said with a smile. "Then everything is settled. You girls have a great vacation, and I'm sure you'll turn in a wonderful project."

"I'm sure they will," Ms. Bailes said, smiling.

When I got home, I ran up to my room to change out of my messy clothes. I went into the laundry room and poured some Stain Out all over my blouse. The instructions said it removed stubborn stains. I hoped that included strawberry juice. Otherwise, I was going to be in big trouble with Momma. The one thing I didn't need any more of was trouble.

I went into the kitchen to ask Momma if I could go over to Caitlin's for a meeting tomorrow. When she found out it was for my social studies project, she said, "No problem."

I called Caitlin and set up a time to meet. I wasn't looking forward to learning about her big fat Greek Christmas, but what choice did I have?

That night, I wrote to Annette, my best friend from Wichita, Kansas, where we used to live. I hadn't heard from her in a month. I was really feeling sad. Lately, nothing seemed to be going right. I really missed having Annette around to talk to about my problems.

Dear Annette,

How are you? I'm not doing so well. You would never believe how hard it is to make good friends here. Not that I'm trying to replace you. You will always be my best friend in the world. I miss you.

What are you getting for Christmas? I had a great wish list going until Momma came up with the idea we should start celebrating Kwanzaa before the baby comes. I forgot to tell you, she's having a baby girl. I have enough trouble with Miss Perfect Sandra. I won't be surprised if this baby can do math problems as soon as she's born!

My grades are better now. Ms. Bailes gave us an assignment to do over the holidays. I need to get an A. I'll let you know what happens.

As you can see, things are going the usual way for me — bad. How is everything with you? What do you want for Christmas? Momma says we have to make handmade gifts this year. Hopefully she will at least let me buy you something from the store.

I don't get the big deal about Kwanzaa. Even if I make something by hand, the stuff I make it with has to be bought from a store! Why can't I just get presents from the store that are already made?

I hope you're doing okay. Write soon! I miss you!

B.F.F.
Love,
Sharie

The next morning, Daddy dropped me off at Caitlin's house. She lives in a beautiful brick mansion with a circular driveway in front. I rang the doorbell. Daddy sat in the car watching me. I was glad it wasn't Momma who drove, or she would probably want to go in, too. Momma loves looking at houses.

A tiny woman in a gray-and-white uniform answered the door.

"Yes, may I help you?" the woman said.

"Hello, I'm Sharie Johnson," I said. "Is Caitlin here?"

"Ah, yes, Miss Sharie. Miss Caitlin is waiting for you in her room. Please come in."

"Thank you," I said as I stepped inside.

Caitlin's house — I mean, mansion — was so huge that I couldn't help but stare. I finally remembered to close my mouth.

A beautiful crystal chandelier hung from the dome-shaped ceiling. A huge vase of flowers sat on a marble table in the center of the room. Down the long halls, on either side of the circular stairway, I could see other rooms filled with beautiful furniture.

"I'm Maria Chase," the woman said with a friendly smile. "I'm Caitlin's nanny."

The only nanny I had ever heard of was Mary Poppins. Caitlin seemed too old to have a nanny. Then I remembered that Caitlin's mother was almost never home, and her dad traveled a lot. I guess Miss Chase took care of Caitlin so she wouldn't be by

66

herself. I started to feel sorry for Caitlin. I would hate it if my momma and daddy were gone all the time.

I followed Miss Chase up a gold-and-white spiral staircase. The strange thing about it was that there weren't any Christmas, decorations anywhere. No tree, no bows, no wreath on the doors, nothing. Caitlin kept making such a big deal about her family's Greek Christmas, I thought there would be Christmas decorations everywhere. Not only was the house not decorated, it was strangely quiet.

We reached the top of the stairs. Then we walked down a long hallway filled with beautiful oil paintings in gold frames. It looked like an art museum.

There was a huge picture of Caitlin at the end of the hall. She was dressed in a long blue gown and was holding a bouquet of white flowers. She wasn't smiling and looked a little bored. Our family pictures were taken at Photomat after church. Sundays are about the only time Daddy wears a suit and I'm clean and in a dress.

The nanny knocked on the door. A muffled voice answered.

"Miss Caitlin," Miss Chase said softly, "your friend is here."

Caitlin opened the door. "Hi there. Come on in."

I just stood in the doorway, staring. You could have put my bedroom and Sandra's bedroom inside Caitlin's room about four times. I had never seen a room so big. Along one wall, there was a flat-screen television and a huge wall of CDs and stereo equipment. On another wall, there were glass cases with rows of dolls, shelves of books, and games. I couldn't believe one kid could have so many things. Caitlin wasn't a movie star, but she lived like one.

I didn't mean to say "wow" so loudly, but I couldn't help myself.

"Your room is incredible," I said.

"Thanks. Have a seat," Caitlin said awkwardly.

I wondered why she was acting so timid. She seemed embarrassed that her house and her room were so big.

"You can sit at that desk over there," Caitlin said.

"I have all my research on the computer and in that folder."

"Would you girls like something to drink or eat?" Miss Chase asked.

"Thanks, that would be great," I said.

"I'll bring up a tray," Miss Chase said. She quietly closed the door.

I stood in front of the computer desk. It was a big-screen computer like I'd seen in high-tech movies. Caitlin pulled over another chair.

"Go on, you can sit in my chair."

I sat down. The chair was bouncy and soft. It was made out of smooth, plastic mesh fabric. It felt great. My desk chair was an old, wooden hand-me-down from the dining room set we had in Kansas. It creaks when I move around on it. That's how Momma knows I'm playing on the computer instead of cleaning my room or sleeping.

"Where's your family?" I asked. "I thought we were going to talk to your mom or interview your dad or something?"

"My father and mother are away," Caitlin said.

Her voice was so soft that I could barely hear her.

"I thought we were going to interview your relatives. How are we going to do this project?"

"We'll research on the computer, then we can write it up."

I stared at her. "You're kidding, right? You think that will get us a good grade? It won't. Ms. Bailes wants more than a plain, old report," I said, feeling really frustrated that I'd come over here for this.

"What do you suggest, then?" she said.

"How about interviewing your mother, your father, and the rest of your family who are coming here for Christmas. If you want, I can come over on Christmas Day, maybe late in the afternoon after we've finished our celebration. I can bring my dad's video camera and we can tape the whole thing. It will be a cool project to show at school."

I had become curious about how the Greeks celebrate Christmas, especially since Caitlin's family had so much money. I thought that if they lived like this every day, they must really have a great time during the holidays.

Caitlin didn't say anything. She sniffed as if she had a cold. She reached inside her sleeve and pulled out her handkerchief. She dabbed at her eyes and her nose. I guess she wasn't feeling well.

"Ms. Bailes said if we combine the projects to show how both of our families celebrate Christmas, we'll get extra points," I said. "My family is celebrating Kwanzaa this year. Maybe you can come over and we can film that, too? What do you think?"

"My father left this morning to go to Greece," Caitlin said stiffly. "My grandmother is very ill and has to have surgery next week. My father won't be coming home until she's better. My mother is in a new play in France. She won't be able to come home until after Christmas."

"Caitlin, we're supposed to research your family's Greek Christmas, remember? It was your idea."

I was starting to get angry. I had gotten into a lot of trouble because Caitlin had insisted on doing this project her way.

"My mother and father will probably be home for New Year's Eve," she said, almost too softly for me to hear. "We're going to celebrate the holidays then."

As usual, I spoke before thinking about it. "New Year's Eve? What about Christmas? Are you going to Greece or to France?"

Chapter Seven

Caitlin's Secret

"Can we change the subject, please?" Caitlin asked.

I could see tears in her eyes. For once, I stopped talking. I swung back and forth in the chair.

"Since my father probably won't be home for Christmas and my mother is working, Maria and I will have Christmas dinner at a hotel."

I couldn't imagine being away from my family at Christmas or celebrating the holiday in a hotel. Caitlin was holding her head down now. I couldn't see her face. "We'll have to do a report on your family's holiday celebration."

I could tell she was crying.

"Okay," I said. "We can do that. I'm sure Ms.

Bailes will understand when she hears about your grandmother."

I was feeling like anything I said would be the wrong thing.

"My parents left me special gifts to open each day until they get back," Caitlin said.

"I don't understand," I said. "What do you mean?"

"They wanted me to have something special to look forward to each day until they get home. So they told Maria to give me one of my presents each day."

"Oh," I said. "What did you get today?"

Caitlin opened her desk drawer. She took out a beautiful gold pen and a red velvet diary with a gold lock.

"That's beautiful," I said.

"Yes," Caitlin said. "My mother gave it to me. She knows how much I like to write. I get to open one of my dad's gifts tomorrow."

I felt terrible. I had been complaining because I wasn't getting any store-bought presents this year.

My parents were taking the time to make gifts for me. Somehow Caitlin's money and her gifts didn't sound so great.

"Can we drop this?" Caitlin said stiffly. "I'm tired of talking about Christmas."

"Sure," I said quickly. "I'll tell you what, let's just think of a way we can report on my family's Christmas and Kwanzaa holidays. Then we can write an outline. How about that?"

"Would you like to have a party?" Caitlin said suddenly.

"A party?" Now I was truly confused.

"When Maria returns with our snacks, we can have a party," Caitlin said, sounding like she did this all the time.

"I suppose," I said, "but don't you think we should at least talk some more about what we plan to do for the project?"

"I don't feel like it," Caitlin said. "I'm tired of talking about Christmas."

"Okay," I said.

"My parents say I'm too old to call Maria my nanny," Caitlin explained. "But I still think of her that way."

"Oh," I said. "I bet it was fun to have a nanny and a mother, too. All we had was our mother."

"I know that," Caitlin said crossly. "You don't have to brag about it. My mother is a very successful European actress, and my father runs a huge corporation. They travel all the time, so I have to have someone to take care of me."

Now I was confused. "Who's bragging?"

"You are," Caitlin snapped back. "Everybody knows your mother comes to school all the time. And your dad always comes to watch every little thing you participate in."

"That's not always such a good thing," I said. "Who wants their parents at their school all the time?"

"I would," Caitlin said. "I would give anything to have my mother come to visit me at school. You know something? Look, uh, if I tell you this, you have to promise not to tell anyone else, okay?"

A tap at the door stopped me from answering.

"Come in," Caitlin said.

Miss Chase came in with a fancy cart decorated with gold roses. "Here are some treats for you and your friend, Caitlin," she said. "I also made some special Greek bread called *christopsomo* and fixed a plate of dried fruits. We used to eat these treats during the holidays when I was a little girl. I used to make them all the time when my children were little."

I noticed that Miss Chase didn't call her Miss Caitlin now. She talked to Caitlin as though they were old friends. I guess that's because they are.

"Don't make a mess, okay, sweeties?" Miss Chase said.

"We won't," Caitlin said. "Thanks."

Miss Chase left, shutting the door behind her.

"What were you going to tell me?" I asked, taking a bite of sandwich cut in the shape of a triangle. "These are cute sandwiches."

"Never mind," Caitlin said. "I don't think telling you is such a good idea."

"We're friends now, aren't we?" I said. "Friends talk to each other."

"You promise not to tell?"

"I promise," I said, "but it's not something bad, is it? My parents don't like it if I keep secrets."

"It's bad to me," Caitlin said, "but I don't think your parents would care if I tell you about it."

"Okay," I said. "Go ahead and tell me."

"Well, sometimes I wish my parents didn't have any money," Caitlin said sadly. "I wouldn't care, as long as they didn't have to work so hard all the time."

I didn't know what to say. Most kids would give anything to have all the things that Caitlin has. I was so used to the way Momma and Daddy are always checking on me and asking about what I'm doing at school that I just took their attention for granted. Sometimes I even wished they'd leave me alone. But I didn't want to be left alone like Caitlin.

"Your dad can't help it if your grandmother is sick, Caitlin. And I'm sure your mother would have made arrangements to be here if she had known you'd be alone at Christmas."

"I know," Caitlin said softly. "But I was really looking forward to having a big family Christmas this year. I knew my mother would be working, but I thought my grandmother and my aunts and uncles were coming to visit. Oh, well. I'll be okay with Maria."

"It will be fun to open your presents every day instead of having to wait. I'd love to eat dinner in a hotel!" I said.

I was trying to make Caitlin feel better, but I don't think I was doing a very good job.

"Yeah, but it's no big deal. We eat out all the time."

"I've never eaten in a hotel. Can you order anything you want?"

"Yes, anything I want," Caitlin said. "I can do anything I want and go anyplace I want. We're going to the 1886 Room at the Driskill Hotel. It's one of the most elegant hotels in Austin."

"Well, this year my momma has decided we're going to start a new tradition of celebrating Kwanzaa. Can you believe it? We're going to make our presents by hand. I hate it. I had a long list of stuff I wanted, but now it's ruined."

"Well, you might like celebrating Kwanzaa," Caitlin said. "I like making things. It sounds like fun to make gifts for one another."

"Do you want to come to my house for the holidays?" I asked. I heard myself saying it, but I couldn't believe it was coming out of my mouth. Of course she wouldn't want to come to our house and watch us open homemade gifts when she could be at the Driskill eating whatever she wanted.

"Do you mean it?" Caitlin asked.

What had I done? Me and my big mouth. I stuttered now. "I, I have to ask my parents first. But sure, if you want to come over . . ."

"I'd like to come," Caitlin said happily. "We could work on our project about your family's Christmas and Kwanzaa celebrations, as long as it's okay with Maria and my parents. Maria will want to meet your mom and dad, too. She was supposed to spend the holidays with her son and his family, but she canceled that to stay with me."

"My parents will want to make sure that you have permission to visit us over the holidays, too." I said.

I wasn't even sure what our Christmas was going to be like now that we were celebrating Kwanzaa, too. It might be too dull and boring for someone like Caitlin.

"Do you want some more juice?" Caitlin asked.

"Sure, why not," I said, holding my glass out. I had never had juice in a crystal goblet before. I had often daydreamed of one day being rich and having everything I wanted. But now, being rich didn't seem so wonderful.

"Let's toast to our friendship," Caitlin said, holding out her glass. "To best friends!"

I held up my glass. "Wait, we can't be best friends. I'm sorry, but I already have two best friends," I said.

Caitlin sighed. "Okay, then. To friendship," she said.

I felt like a rat. She looked so sad. But I couldn't say I was her best friend. I had promised Annette that she'd always be my best friend. Then there was Hannah. I couldn't betray Hannah. Caitlin was always saying mean things about Hannah, or excluding her from things. No, I wouldn't be a traitor. I said, "To friendship and project partners."

We clinked our glasses and drank our juice. Then we cleaned up. I called my dad to pick me up.

I played on Caitlin's computer while I waited for Daddy to arrive. Caitlin and I didn't talk much. We sort of ran out of things to say. She just sat in her rocking chair, looking out the window. When Daddy rang the doorbell, I almost tripped trying to get out of there.

"How did it go?" he asked me when I got in the car.

"Better than I thought," I said. "Daddy, would you and Momma ever leave me and Sandra alone at Christmastime? I mean, what if you won a cruise or something and only the two of you could go?"

He glanced over at me. "Don't be crazy, of course not. It's never going to happen, mate. Knowing your mother, when you're fifty years old, she'll still expect you at our dinner table for Christmas."

"No problem, Daddy," I said. "I was just wondering, that's all."

Suddenly, I felt much better. I looked back at Caitlin's house. It still looked huge even though we were far away from it.

When it was time for dinner, I dreaded bringing up my invitation to Caitlin to spend the holidays with us. But I also knew that Momma and Daddy hate last-minute surprises. Sandra does, too. I was the only one who waits until the last minute.

"Momma, I have a little problem," I said, scooping up some mashed potatoes.

"What is it, honey? Please don't tell me you don't want to do the project with Caitlin."

"It's not that, Momma," I said. "Actually, we've decided to do the project on our family's holiday."

Daddy stopped cutting his steak. "What did you say?"

"That's a great idea," Momma said. "I'm glad you two are getting along."

"It was my idea for her to make friends with Caitlin," Sandra said.

"Yes, we're friends now," I said.

"Tell us about your project," Daddy said, putting his steak knife down. He folded his hands under his chin. "Go on and tell us about it."

"Well, she wants to come over here for the holidays and celebrate with us," I said hurriedly. "She also wants to spend Kwanzaa with us. That way, we'll be able to do a better report."

"What?" Momma said. "What about her family's Christmas plans? Her parents won't want her over here when she should be with them. My goodness, you children can be so inconsiderate sometimes."

"Your momma is right," Daddy said. "She needs to spend Christmas with her family."

"I'm sure she didn't mean she wanted to come over Christmas morning or anything," Momma said. "She probably just wants to stop over late on Christmas Day. Right, Sharie?"

"No, she'd like to spend Christmas Eve and Christmas Day with us. She also wants to celebrate some of the Kwanzaa holiday with us," I said.

Momma said, "And her parents will agree to that?"

"She says they will. They're not going to be home, anyway."

"What do you mean?" Daddy said. "Then how is she coming over here? I don't understand."

"Her parents are out of the country," I said. "Her grandmother lives in Greece and needs emergency surgery. Her father will probably stay with her grandmother until a few days after Christmas. Caitlin's mother is in a play in France. Her parents left her nanny in charge of her."

"The poor thing," Momma said. "Of course she can come over here for the holidays. Just call her after dinner so that I can speak with her nanny to make sure she has permission."

"Okay, thanks," I said. "I'll call her. She'll be so happy."

"Oh, that's too bad," Sandra said sadly. "I'd hate to be alone at Christmastime."

I wasn't at all sure about this. I didn't want anything else to ruin my Christmas, and sometimes Caitlin was hard to handle. Her moods changed with the wind, and Caitlin could be temperamental, spoiled, and rude when she wanted to be. Come to think of it, that's probably why Ms. Bailes said that we're so much alike. I would keep my fingers crossed that things would work out for the best. But let's face it, in Sharie Johnson's world, they rarely do.

Chapter Eight

What Is Kwanzaa, Anyway?

The first problem started as we cleared the table.

"Sharie," Momma said, "I have been so busy I haven't done my homework about Kwanzaa yet. Since you're going to report on it, why don't you do it for me? Sandra is going to visit her friends tonight."

"Oh, Momma," I wailed. "I was going to play video games tonight, since there's no school tomorrow. Can't it wait until Caitlin comes over so we can work on it together? Sandra is the one who wants to do the Kwanzaa thing. Make her do it."

"I have my own school project to do," Sandra said.

"Come on, Sharie. It might be interesting," Daddy

88

said. "If you can't get enough information, then Sandra can help you."

I gave up. "Alright, I'll look it up."

I searched my shelf for a book I had about Kwanzaa titled *Seven Spools of Thread*. I had gotten it last year at a Kwanzaa party thrown by some friends of my parents. The book had a lot of information about the holiday. I had enjoyed reading it. The art was so alive, it seemed to jump off the page.

Then I got on the Internet. I started reading information about Kwanzaa. The more I read, the happier I became. Maybe this would work out. According to my research, Kwanzaa worked best when it was not mixed with any other celebration. And Kwanzaa began the day after Christmas. I stopped reading and printed out the pages of information. Wow! What a stroke of luck. I ran into the kitchen with the papers. Momma was sitting at the table studying a recipe card.

"Guess what, Momma!" I said, almost bursting to get it out.

She looked up. "What is it, Sharie?"

"We aren't supposed to combine Kwanzaa with Christmas. First off, it doesn't even start until after Christmas. And there's something else you need to know. Let me read this to you."

Momma put down her recipe card and gave me her full attention. "Go ahead and read it to me."

"Okay, here are some questions someone asked. 'Can people celebrate Kwanzaa and Christmas? Is Kwanzaa an alternative to Christmas?'"

"Those are interesting questions," Momma said. "What are the answers?"

"'Kwanzaa was not created to give people an alternative to their own religion or religious holiday. Instead, it's a common ground of African culture.' See, Momma, we should go ahead and buy our Christmas presents like always," I said.

"I never said we wouldn't," Momma said. "You just got so worked up about making presents that I didn't say anything. I thought I'd surprise you on Christmas morning."

"Oh, Momma!" I laughed. "You sure had me fooled!"

"See," Momma said, "I've always told you to do your research before you make decisions about things. Now that you've had time to research Kwanzaa, do you see why we want to start celebrating the holiday?"

"Yes, ma'am," I said. "And best of all, since we're celebrating both holidays this year, I get even more presents!"

"Are presents all that the holidays mean to you? We've spoiled both you girls too much."

"No, you haven't," I said. "We're not spoiled. If you want to see spoiled, you should see Caitlin's room. She has everything! I can't believe one person has so many beautiful things, Momma."

"Well, beautiful things aren't always the answer," Momma said. "I think everyone will enjoy making gifts for Kwanzaa. It will be a new experience for Caitlin, too."

"I can't make good gifts," I said. "Sandra doesn't mind making the presents because she's good at things like that."

Sandra walked in and grabbed a drink out of the refrigerator.

"What am I good at?" Sandra asked.

I rolled my eyes. "You just want to hear us brag about you," I said.

"So, what's wrong with that?" Sandra asked.

"Sandra, you're just in time to help us plan our holiday celebrations. Sharie says that we should celebrate Christmas like we always have, and then celebrate Kwanzaa."

"Whatever you want to do is fine with me," Sandra said sweetly.

"Terrific!" Momma said. "You did some great research on the subject, Sharie."

"Thank you, Momma," I said, beaming.

"Why don't you read us more about Kwanzaa? What kinds of decorations do we need?" Momma asked.

"Okay, it says here that we need *Mazao*. Those are the crops. That means we need something that symbolizes the harvest celebration. We can put out a basket of fruits and vegetables to represent that. Then we need *Mkeka*, which is the mat. It symbolizes the foundation. Everything sits on top of it. *Kinara* is the candleholder. It holds seven candles to represent the seven days of Kwanzaa."

"What color are the candles?" Sandra asked.

I made a face. I was sure she asked because she knew I didn't know the answer. She always researches every last bit of information she can find. I try to do as little as possible. "I'll have to look that up," I said.

"That's okay," Momma said. "Go on."

"*Muhindi*, that's the corn. It represents the children." I giggled. "That's weird."

"What's so weird about it?" Momma asked.

"Well, you know, it's funny to picture kids as corn!" I laughed.

Sandra laughed, too. "She's right, Momma. Can you see us as yellow corn?"

"Yeah," I said, cracking up now.

"Okay, that's enough," Momma said. "Please go on, Sharie."

"*Mishumaa Saba* — those are the seven candles," I said, still stifling my giggles. "And no, I don't know the colors. The candles represent the seven principles. We'll also need a *Kikombe cha Umoja*, meaning the unity cup, for unity."

"There's a lot more to Kwanzaa than I thought," Momma said. "What are the gifts called?"

"*Zawadi*," I read. "That's the word for gifts. The last thing is the flag, called the *Bendera*. It's black, red, and green. The candles are the same colors, I'll bet."

"You're probably right," Momma agreed. "I can't wait until the celebration starts."

"I can't wait until Christmas so I can get at least one of the presents on my Christmas list," I said.

"I told you not to worry about Christmas," Sandra said. "You were all upset over nothing, see?"

"Yeah, I know," I said. "But everything has been changing so fast that it's making my head spin."

"Well, hang on," Sandra said. "There are more changes coming!"

She grabbed me by the arm and spun me around. I giggled. I was so dizzy that I collapsed in the middle of the floor. Sandra fell down next to me.

"You two sure are silly tonight," Momma said.

"Aren't you supposed to go to Hannah's tomorrow for the first night of Hanukkah?"

"Yes, ma'am," I said, "but I don't really want to go."

"It's too late now. You already agreed. Your daddy will drop you off and come back to pick you up."

"Okay, Momma, but do I have to wear a dress?"

"No, you can wear some nice pants and a blouse," Momma said.

Thank goodness. Sometimes she forces me to wear a dress. The doorbell rang.

"That's Jennie. I've got to go now. Good night," Sandra said, whispering as she passed by me. "Hope you get a bug bite."

"Momma," I said.

"Yes?"

"Nothing," I said. I wasn't going to fall for it this time. Momma didn't hear Sandra, and Sandra would just make up something that sounded like what she'd said. Like "sleep tight." It wasn't worth tattling. I had to admit it, though: Sandra really helped me out with Caitlin. Her advice to make friends with Caitlin worked.

Now, if I can just get through tomorrow. It wouldn't be so bad if it were just Hannah and me, but Anysa would be there. I wondered if she was as nice as Hannah said.

The next morning, I played on the computer for a long time. I love my computer. It was my Christmas gift last year. I write all my plays and poems on it. I love using it for research.

I looked up some information about Hanukkah. It turns out that Hanukkah is an eight-day celebration. Hannah had tried explaining to me the history of the Jewish people and what Hanukkah means. She said that she loves celebrating Hanukkah. Maybe it would be fun. I'd find out soon enough.

After I finished getting dressed, I hopped into the car with Daddy.

• "Do you know any Jewish people, Daddy? Were there Jewish people in the navy?"

"Of course," Daddy said. "Don't you remember Sergeant and Mrs. Katz from the naval base?"

"Yes, but I didn't know they were Jewish."

"Are you excited about going to Hannah's?"

"Excited? Why would I be excited, Daddy?"

"You're having a new experience! When I was a kid, I always wanted to explore the world, meet new people, do things I'd read about in books. Back in our little town, almost everyone was the same race or religion."

"I don't think much about stuff like that," I said.

"Maybe someday you will. That's partly why I joined the navy. I wanted to travel, see the world, give my children a wider view of life."

"Well, you did, Daddy," I said with a smile.

I couldn't believe he was talking to me like a grown-up. I felt like giving him a hug. Daddy was telling me about his childhood dreams. I don't know if I'd ever thought about what Daddy was like as a kid. Maybe he was a lot like Sandra. Or was he more like me? I smiled at the thought of my neat, orderly father having a junky room, dirty clothes, and papers scattered everywhere when he was young.

"Glad to see you smiling. I know the last few months have been pretty hard on you, Sharie," Daddy said. "A lot of changes have happened to you. First we moved, then you had to enroll in a new school and make new friends, and now your momma is having a baby and we're celebrating a new holiday. But you know what?"

"What?" I said. Here it comes. I bet he's going to say I should have done better in school or something. Or maybe he's going to say how easy it is for Sandra to adjust to everything without complaining like I do.

"You're a great kid," Daddy said. "You roll with the punches, but not without speaking up for yourself. I like that. Now, here we are."

I was speechless. Daddy said he liked it when I spoke up for myself. He didn't scold me or say I talk too much. He said he liked it. I hugged him when I got out of the car. "Thank you, Daddy," I said.

He kissed me on the forehead. "No, thank you, baby. Now, go have fun!"

Chapter Nine

Happy Hanukkah!

Hannah opened the door. "Hey, Sharie! *Hag Sameach!* That means 'happy holiday!' Come on in."

Hannah was wearing one of her wild outfits. This time, she had on every color known to man. I blinked.

"Wow, you have on a lot of different colors."

"The better to see them," she said, laughing like she wasn't embarrassed at all. That's what I like about her the most. She wore what she wanted and didn't worry if others made fun of her. Sometimes I don't dress so neatly, but I still care what people think about me. Not enough to change it, though.

Anysa came into the living room. Anysa is a pretty, tall, dark-skinned girl with beautiful hair.

"Hi, Sharie," Anysa said. "Come join us! We're having fun."

"Yeah," Hannah said. "Come on, my mom's waiting for you to get this party started."

"Great," I said. I ran after them into the living room.

"Hello, Sharie," Mrs. Lowenstein said. "I'm glad you could make it! Okay, girls! The first thing we're going to do is sing. Here are the words."

Mrs. Lowenstein began passing out sheets of paper. We began to sing, following her tune:

Hanukkah, O Hanukkah, come light the menorah.
Let's have a party, we'll all dance the horah.
Gather 'round the table, we'll give you a treat.
Dreidels to play with and latkes to eat.

"Very good," Mrs. Lowenstein said, clapping her hands. "Now I'm going to finish making the food. Go ahead, girls! Have some fun and then we'll eat."

"Okay, now, let's play ball," Hannah said.

"Ball?" I said. "We're going to play ball?"

Hannah laughed. "Nope, I just always wanted to say that. We're going to play the dreidel game."

"What's that?" Anysa asked.

"Yeah," I said. "What's that?"

Hannah showed us a four-sided top. Its sides were marked by four letters of the Hebrew alphabet: nun, gimel, hay, and shin. Hannah explained that the letters mean, "A great miracle happened here."

"Take these," Hannah said, passing out pieces of candy. "Divide them among us. They'll be our gelt. Each person places one gelt in the center of the circle. We take turns spinning the dreidel. If it falls on the Hebrew letter nun, the player gets nothing. If it's on the letter gimel, the player takes all the ante, that's the candy in the center of the circle."

"Then what?" Anysa asked.

"Then we all put another piece of candy in the center."

"This seems like fun," I said. I gave the dreidel a spin.

"It is fun," Hannah said. "Now, if the dreidel falls

on the letter hay, you get half of the center pot. If it's on the letter shin, you put in one ante from your stash."

"So how do you win?" I asked.

"The winner is the one who has the most gelt at the end of the game."

"When does the game end?" Anysa asked. "I mean, how do you decide who's the winner?"

"We can decide now," Hannah said. "Let's say that we end the game when my mother calls us to come into the kitchen."

"What are we going to do in the kitchen?" I asked.

"It's a surprise," Hannah said. "Are you ready to play?"

"Yes!" we screamed.

I loved this game. I was winning. By the time Mrs. Lowenstein called us into the kitchen, I had a pile of candy.

"Come on, girls. We're going to make some latkes from scratch."

"What's that?" I asked. Not something with spinach, I hoped. Latkes sounded kind of spinachy.

"I don't like spinach."

"No, latkes don't have spinach in them," Mrs. Lowenstein said. "They're potato pancakes. You're going to love them."

"They're good," Anysa said. "I've had them before."

"Wash your hands, girls, and let's start cooking," Mrs. Lowenstein said.

We washed and dried our hands and put on aprons. Mrs. Lowenstein put some oil into a frying pan. Then we mixed together shredded potatoes, onion, eggs, and cracker crumbs in a bowl. We made little mounds with the mixture and pressed them flat with a spatula. We fried them in a pan until they were golden brown on both sides. We took turns flipping them over.

"Would you like to try one?" Mrs. Lowenstein asked.

"Sure," I said.

Mrs. Lowenstein put a latke, a little applesauce, and a dollop of sour cream on a plate for me to sample. I took a big bite. It was delicious!

After we finished cooking our latkes, we went into

the dining room. Hannah and Mrs. Lowenstein had decorated it with six-pointed Jewish stars, and little dreidels hung on a string.

"Now we're going to start the Hanukkah celebration," Mrs. Lowenstein said.

She lit a candle on the candleholder, which she called a menorah. Then she recited some words. I couldn't understand them, but they sounded pretty nice. Mrs. Lowenstein told me that she was speaking Hebrew. She explained the meaning of Hanukkah. This holiday was turning out to be better than I had expected. We had a delicious dinner, and then we sang more songs and played with the dreidel again.

When Daddy came to pick me up, I didn't want to go home. I was having fun, and I really liked Anysa, just like Hannah said I would. We all hugged before I got in the car. Anysa was spending the night. I asked if I could spend the night, too. Daddy said I needed to come home. I started to argue, but then I decided to just quietly get in the car. I didn't want to ruin the evening by being stubborn.

I told Momma and Daddy all about Hanukkah

at Hannah's house. Sandra was spending the night at a friend's house. They were happy I'd learned so much about Jewish traditions and that I had had such a good time. I don't know why I was dreading celebrating Hanukkah with Hannah. I almost cheated myself out of a lot of fun. From now on, I need to open up my mind to new cultural experiences, just like Daddy said.

Finally, it was time to go to bed. I hugged and kissed Momma and Daddy good night. I had fun talking to them without Sandra being there. This is what it must be like to be an only child.

Daddy said he would fix some of his famous blueberry pancakes with pecans on top in the morning. I went to bed feeling happier than I had felt in a long time. I fell asleep with a smile on my face.

The next morning, I gobbled down my pancakes. They were delicious. One thing about Daddy, he can cook as good as Momma does. I looked at him and Momma. They were like two little kids, teasing each other and laughing together. I was lucky to have them for parents.

The telephone rang. Momma answered it.

"It's for you, Sharie."

I raced to the phone, hoping it was Hannah. I wanted to tell her again what a good time I'd had at her house.

"Hello?"

"Hello, traitor," Caitlin said.

"What? Caitlin, what are you talking about?"

"I called Anysa to ask her if she could come over. Her mother said she was at Hannah's house. I called her at Hannah's and she told me you were there last night, too."

"So?" I said.

"Not only are you and Hannah trying to steal Anysa from me, but now you're choosing them over me, too."

"What are you talking about? When did I choose anyone? Why don't you have Miss Chase take you over to Hannah's house? Hannah loves company."

"I told you!" Caitlin shouted. "I don't like Hannah. Anysa knows that. I told her not to go over there."

"Caitlin, don't you remember? Anysa and Hannah are doing their project together. Besides, you can't tell anyone who to be friends with."

"I can do whatever I please," Caitlin said. "I knew you were trying to trick me into thinking you liked me. But you don't. I bet you were all talking about me."

"You're wrong. Your name never came up. What is wrong with you? I can't believe you're acting like this. You're just causing trouble!"

"Me? Causing trouble? You're the one who's always causing trouble."

"Yeah, that's true, and unfortunately it usually has something to do with you," I said. "But you know what?"

"What?"

"I'm done trying to be friends with you. I don't see how someone with everything can be so mean and unhappy. 'Bye."

I hung up. My hands were shaking. I couldn't believe that girl. I called Hannah.

"Do you know that Caitlin called here and accused me of being a traitor because I'm friends with you and Anysa?"

"I know. She called here and yelled at Anysa. Hold on, I'll let you talk to her."

"Hi, Sharie," Anysa said. She sounded awfully calm to have just been yelled at.

"I'm so mad at Caitlin," I said. "Aren't you?"

"No, I feel sorry for her," Anysa said softly.

"Sorry? I don't feel sorry for Caitlin," I said.

"You and Hannah just don't understand her, that's all. Once you get to know her, you'll feel differently about her," Anysa said. "She's had a hard time."

"Are you serious?" I said. "She has everything she wants. I'll never feel sorry for her."

"My mom always says 'never say never,'" Anysa said. "Just wait. You'll like her once you get to know her. Aren't you doing your project with her?"

"Yes, and she's supposed to come spend some of the holidays with us."

"Just give her a chance," Anysa said. "Have you ever felt that your family didn't care?"

I didn't answer. But I had to admit that I did feel that way. Especially now, with Momma getting ready to have a baby.

"Sharie?" Anysa said. "Are you still there?"

"I'm listening," I said.

"Caitlin talks without thinking sometimes. Do you understand?" Anysa said.

Boy, did I ever. I talk without thinking most of the time.

"Yeah, but I don't have to like it," I said. "I'll talk to you later."

"Okay, 'bye!" Anysa said. "Have fun with Caitlin during the holidays."

"I'll try," I said.

"Try to be nice to her," Anysa said. "She really needs a friend right now."

"Okay," I said.

Chapter Ten

All the Things That Money Can't Buy

I hung up the phone and went into the living room. Today we were going to decorate for Christmas. Sandra came home just in time to help unpack the decorations. She kept talking about how much fun she had had at her friend Jennie's house. I didn't say anything. I was too busy thinking about what Anysa had said about Caitlin.

Momma makes a big deal about getting ready for the holidays. She even sends each one of us an invitation, which she makes herself, to invite us to the Christmas tree-trimming party. We sing carols, dance, eat cookies, and string rows and rows of glass beads and popcorn.

Momma usually puts the angel on top of the tree. But this year, Daddy did it. He said that from now on, we should all take turns putting the angel on the tree. Soon, the new baby would be taking her turn, too. Momma said she thinks our tree-trimming party is one of the best parts of the holidays. I used to say it was for little kids and that we're too old now for all that stuff. But now I'm not so sure about that. I would miss it if we stopped having our little party every year.

Daddy went to pick up Caitlin. She was staying over for Christmas Eve, Christmas Day, and the first day of the Kwanzaa celebration. I tried to get my room cleaned up. I put away most of my books and clothes, but some things I just stuffed under my bed. I was sure she wouldn't look under there.

Caitlin arrived with fancy leather luggage. I usually put all my stuff in my backpack or in one of Daddy's old duffel bags when I'm going to someone's house.

"Hello," Caitlin said.

"Hi," I said. We just looked at each other.

"Sharie, take your guest upstairs so she can put away her things," Momma said. "We're so happy you're going to be spending the holidays with us, Caitlin. I hope you enjoy yourself."

Momma gave Caitlin a big hug and patted her gently on the cheek.

"Thank you for inviting me," Caitlin said softly.

I took Caitlin upstairs and showed her my room. She was going to have to sleep on the little foldout cot we keep for guests. Hannah slept on it all the time, but it bothered me to have Caitlin sleep there. I knew she wasn't used to such a small bed.

I thought she would say something smart about how small my room was compared to hers. Actually, you could almost put *all* of our bedrooms into her room. But she didn't make fun of me.

"You have a nice bedroom," Caitlin said politely.

"Thanks," I said stiffly.

"Sharie, are you going to be mad at me the entire time I'm here?" Caitlin asked.

"Well, you started it," I said.

Did she think I was just supposed to forget that she yelled at me and called me a traitor?

"I'm sorry about the other day," Caitlin said. "I really am. Sometimes I say things I don't mean."

"Okay, I understand," I said.

Momma walked in. "Girls, it's time to make the gifts. Let's go downstairs, okay? Your daddy has everything ready to go."

Oh, no. I don't believe Momma would allow Daddy to help us. Now, instead of making crafts that were boring, they would be boring *and* hard.

Daddy liked everything all neat and lined up. I mean, you couldn't just toss the glue onto the table or throw paper down. You had to close everything up after you used it, put things back in order, and not make a huge mess. He and Sandra usually had a ball because that's how they were all the time. I'm so messy that arts-and-crafts projects are never fun for me.

I looked at Caitlin. She seemed perfectly happy about the whole idea. That's probably because she didn't know how strict Daddy is about everything. I smiled to myself. For once, Caitlin isn't going to get her way. We marched downstairs behind Momma into the kitchen.

"All right, shipmates," Daddy said. "Let's do this quickly and properly. Caitlin, you and Sharie are over there at that table, Sandra and Momma are here, and I am on point."

That meant he'd be walking from table to table straightening everything up.

Daddy had set the tables. They were lined with papers, colorful cloths, beads, and glue.

"I think I'll make a friendship bracelet," Sandra said. "I saw this pretty bracelet in one of Momma's craft books."

Momma had checked out a stack of arts-and-crafts books from the library. Sandra and Momma had spent last week looking through them. I just ignored them. I hate making crafts.

Daddy came over to our table. "What are you girls making?"

"It's a secret," I said. "I'm making something for Momma."

I got some glue, a handful of buttons, and a mirror. I started gluing the buttons onto it.

"What about you, Caitlin?" Daddy said.

"I'm making something for my mother, too. I've never done anything like this before. We always buy our Christmas presents."

Caitlin started gluing some brightly colored pieces of yarn to the top of a plain wooden box. I thought Caitlin was bragging about always buying their Christmas gifts. I was getting ready to say something smart until I looked at her face. She was smiling. She was actually enjoying herself. I couldn't believe it. It seemed like I learned something new about Caitlin every day.

"I'm sure that your parents will treasure anything you make," Daddy said. "Wait, let me show you something!" Daddy practically ran out of the room.

I thought, *Please don't embarrass me, Daddy*. I was pretty sure he was going to get one of the pretty gifts Sandra had made for him when she was a little girl. She was always making him something.

Daddy returned, holding something behind his back.

"Recognize this?" he asked.

I dropped my head. Oh, no. I'd made it for him while he was at sea. I couldn't believe he still had that ugly thing.

"Nobody knows what that horrible thing is, Daddy," I said.

"Oh, baby," Daddy said. "It's not ugly to me. The important thing is that you made it with your own little hands. You were just seven years old. It was the first thing you ever made for me. At first, I wasn't sure what it was, but you know what? I didn't care. My daughter made it. I was proudly showing it to some of my boys on the ship, and they were the ones who told me what it was."

"Well, what is it?" Sandra asked. "It's kind of hard to tell."

To tell the truth, I wasn't sure what it was, either. It had been so long ago. It looked terrible. I glanced at Caitlin to see if she was laughing. She was smiling at Daddy. She looked like she was enjoying his story.

"It's to hang my medals on. See, it's in the shape of a naval submarine. I hang my medals on these little hooks. I love it."

I couldn't believe my ears. It did look like a submarine now that Daddy said it. I had made something he loved. Something even more special than the cute little things Sandra made.

"I love this because it's practical, it's useful, and it means something," Daddy said.

"What about the things I've made for you, Daddy?" Sandra said.

"I love anything my children make," Daddy said. "So you see, Caitlin, your parents will love whatever you make. If it came from a store, it wouldn't be as special. Anyone can go to a store and buy something. But to make something from your heart, that's really special."

Caitlin started to cry.

"What's the matter, honey?" Momma said, running over to hug her.

"It's, it's just that I feel so ashamed," Caitlin said.

"Ashamed?" Daddy asked.

"Yes. I wish I had a family like yours."

I couldn't move. Could she have said what I thought she said? She wanted a family like mine? My family was making handmade Kwanzaa gifts. I always thought that it would be wonderful to be able to buy everything on my Christmas wish list and to have lots of money like Caitlin. Now I wasn't so sure.

"I really miss my parents," Caitlin said. "We were really looking forward to the holidays this year. My grandmother, my aunts, and my cousins were supposed to come to America for the first time. We had hired someone to decorate the house, and we were going to have a big party. I'm really worried about my grandmother."

"I'm sure your grandmother will be fine," Momma said. "Your nanny told me that your father and mother will be calling you here every night. Don't worry, okay?"

"Okay," Caitlin said. "I'm sorry. I don't want it to seem like I'm not happy to be here. I'm having fun and everything looks so pretty. Who decorated your tree?"

We all just looked at one another. There was no way anyone wanted to talk about how much fun we had at our little tree-trimming party.

Finally, Daddy said, "I think it's time we all had some hot cocoa."

"Yes, Daddy's right," Momma said. "Let's have some cocoa and take a break."

We sat around sipping cocoa. No one was talking much. Not even big mouth me. I didn't know what to say. I used to sort of envy Caitlin. Now I was beginning to feel differently. A rich girl with everything she could want envied us. Would wonders never cease?

I looked at Caitlin and all my bad feelings about her melted away. Now I understood what Anysa meant. I felt sorry for Caitlin. There were things money couldn't buy, and I had them all.

Chapter Eleven

Merry Christmas and Happy Kwanzaa!

On Christmas morning, my parents surprised all of us. When we came downstairs, there was a pile of presents under the tree. Sandra grinned when I opened the present from her. It was a CD I'd been wanting. It had been on my wish list.

Sandra and I both got lots of things from our lists. Not everything, of course; we never got everything on our lists. But it was enough.

Momma and Daddy had bought Caitlin some presents, too, so she wouldn't feel left out. They were little things, like a charm to go on her bracelet and some bubble bath. She acted as though they had bought her the world. She seemed really happy about it.

Daddy cooked his famous pancakes, and we all laughed and talked until noon. Then Caitlin and I filmed each other around the house. The entire day was nothing but fun and games.

Caitlin's father and mother called to wish her a merry Christmas, and she talked to each of them for a long time. She kept telling them how much fun she was having. Caitlin's mom talked to Momma for a while. Momma acted like they were old friends.

Daddy had a chance to talk with Caitlin's dad. Caitlin's grandmother was doing much better. Daddy was smiling when he hung up the phone.

"Why are you smiling so much, Daddy?" I asked.

"It's a surprise," Daddy said. "Come on, it's time to play games."

I wanted to ask him more questions, but I knew what he would say: "If I tell you, it won't be a surprise."

We played board games for the rest of the night. Then Daddy made hot cocoa. We sat in the living room and looked at the lights twinkling on the Christmas tree. Daddy told story after story about Christmastime when we were little girls. Caitlin laughed until she almost cried at some of the silly things we did to find out where our gifts were hidden. Finally, it was time to go to bed. I really didn't want the night to end. It had been one of the best Christmases ever.

Caitlin and I got ready for bed, but we didn't go to sleep. We talked and giggled for hours. It was late when Daddy finally came down the hall and shut out the lights.

"Lights out, mates," Daddy said.

"Good night, Daddy," I said.

"Good night, Mr. Johnson," Caitlin said.

" 'Night, mates," Daddy said.

"This has been one of the best holidays I've had in a long time," Caitlin whispered after Daddy was gone.

It was dark, so I couldn't see her face, but her voice didn't sound like she was making fun of us. I think she really meant it.

"Good," I said. "We're glad you could come."

"I'm glad I came, too," Caitlin said.

I rolled over and tried to fall asleep. I kept thinking about something Momma always says: "Money isn't everything." I finally drifted off to sleep.

The next day, we rolled out of bed and headed downstairs. I knew it would be a long day the minute we walked into the kitchen.

Daddy said, "*Habari Gani,*" to Momma, Sandra, Caitlin, and me. We all stood there staring back at him.

"Come on," he said. "You're supposed to say '*Umoja.*'"

Momma, Sandra, and Caitlin said, "*Umoja.*"

I rolled my eyes and mumbled, "*Umoja,* whatever." I was always in a grumpy mood in the morning if I stayed up late the night before.

"I didn't hear you, Sharie," Daddy said, still smiling.

"*Umoja,*" I yawned.

Daddy said, "Now, that's the spirit!"

"The first thing we do is say a prayer," Daddy said, holding out his hands.

I blinked and plopped down in a chair. "Okay."

"No, we're supposed to stand," Daddy said.

No one seemed to be tired but me. I was the only one sitting down.

"Who said we're supposed to stand?" I asked. "I didn't read that in the papers I gave you and Momma."

"I found my own instructions about Kwanzaa, and we're going to follow them," Daddy said. "So please stand up."

I could tell he was getting upset, so I stood up quickly. We held hands while Daddy said a prayer. Then, just when we thought he was finished, he threw his right arm up into the air, open-handed, and then pulled it down, closing it into a fist and yelling, "*Harambee!*"

I jumped. He screamed so loud he scared me. I stared at him like he had lost his mind. Everyone else laughed.

"Okay, everyone do what you just saw me do. And we'll all shout '*Harambee*' together. We're going to do it seven times. Come on, *Harambee!*"

He looked so cheerful about it that we all just followed him. Of course, my *Harambee* wasn't as loud as everyone else's. Caitlin was the loudest, and I know she didn't even know what *Harambee* meant. Of course, neither did I. I wouldn't have to wonder for long.

"What does *Harambee* mean, Mr. Johnson?" Caitlin asked.

I shut my eyes. Oh, no, here we go. I hoped Daddy was going to give her a short answer and not a long lecture about Kwanzaa.

"*Harambee* means, 'Let's pull together.' It's a call for unity, to work together and struggle for the family."

"Can we eat now?" I asked.

"May we," Momma corrected me. "Sure, let's eat."

Momma cooked eggs, bacon, toast, and grits. It was delicious, as always. Caitlin seemed to love it. She even mopped up the grits that were left in her bowl with her toast, like Daddy does. I laughed so hard I started to choke. I gulped down my glass of milk.

"What's so funny?" Caitlin asked.

"Yes, please share with us so we can laugh, too," Daddy said.

"That girl has cleaned her plate so shiny we won't even have to wash it," I said.

Daddy and Momma gave me the you-better-be-quiet look.

Caitlin stared at me. She looked embarrassed.

Me and my big mouth! I wish I hadn't said anything.

"Don't pay any attention to Sharie, Caitlin. She normally cleans her plate the same way you did. And it's a compliment to the chef!" Momma said.

Caitlin looked like she was about to cry.

Daddy said, "Sharie was just teasing you. Apologize to Caitlin, Sharie. What you said hurt her feelings."

"Gosh, I was only playing. It was a joke."

Tears swelled in Caitlin's eyes. I knew then that there was no winning this one. I should have kept my big mouth shut. "I'm sorry, Caitlin."

"That's okay," Caitlin said.

Deep down, I was mad that I had to apologize. If

Sandra had said the same thing, I bet they wouldn't have said one word. I bet they would have just told Caitlin that Sandra was just playing around and left it at that. But no, because it's me, I have to apologize.

I asked to be excused.

"You're going to miss singing the Kwanzaa song."

I stared at him. Was he for real? I went to my room. I could hear them singing the stupid song that I didn't want to sing, anyway. I flopped down on my bed. I guess I must have fallen back asleep. The next thing I knew, someone was knocking on my door.

"Come in," I said.

"Hey, pumpkin," Daddy said. "Are you all right?"

"Yeah, I'm okay," I said. "I'm just tired. Why do you have your coat on?"

"It's a secret. I'll be back shortly. And when I come back, I'll have a surprise for you," he said, grinning.

"Okay," I said. Daddy was full of surprises this week.

"Here's your buddy," Daddy said, moving out of the doorway to let Caitlin pass.

"Are you all right?" Caitlin asked.

"Yeah, I'm always grumpy when I'm sleepy," I said. "I didn't mean to hurt your feelings. I really was joking, honest."

"That's okay," Caitlin said.

"Haven't you ever had grits before?" I asked.

"No," she smiled. "I don't care what you say. Those grits were good and I was going to eat every bite!"

"Girls," Momma called, "go on and get dressed. We need to get ready to go to the Kwanzaa celebration."

Caitlin and I covered our mouths to smother our giggles. We hurried to get ready.

After we dressed, Momma started telling us about the things they had planned for Kwanzaa. Caitlin was much more excited than I was.

"I'll go get the camera so we can film everything," Caitlin said. "Make sure you take good notes, Sharie. Our report is going to be great!"

"Surprise!" Daddy shouted. He walked through the door with Hannah and Anysa right behind him.

"In the holiday spirit, I thought it'd be a good idea to bring you girls together," said Daddy.

At first, things were a little tense. I guess Hannah was still upset about what Caitlin had said to her. We went into my room, and soon we were all laughing and talking.

"Girls, come on. It's time to go to the Kwanzaa ceremony," Momma said.

We all raced downstairs and piled into the van. On the way, Daddy told us about the meaning of Kwanzaa. Caitlin and I smiled at each other. Once we got to the center, we admired the pretty decorations. There were several families there from our church.

Caitlin and I filmed everything for our project. I also took notes.

Everyone had a part to play in the ceremony.

Sandra walked over to the piano. She was the talent of our family, of course. She played the Kwanzaa song. I couldn't believe that she had learned it that fast. Daddy just taught it to her the other day, but that's Sandra. She can play just about anything.

My duty was to light the black candle for the principle of the first day, unity, or *Umoja*. Caitlin filmed me. After I lit the candle, each person said something about the principle of unity. I took the camera from Caitlin.

"Good job," she said as she sat down next to me.

"Thanks," I said.

A group of dancers dressed in African-style clothing marched out. A long line of drummers took their places behind drums of various sizes.

The drummers beat out a song. The dancers stood still for a moment. Then they suddenly exploded into a beautiful dance. I was so busy looking at the dancers that I almost forgot to adjust the camera. I focused the camera and looked at Caitlin to see if she was taking notes. She looked funny. I leaned over and whispered, "What's the matter with you?"

She said, "I don't think I've ever been the minority before. It's a little uncomfortable to stand out like this."

The only white people at the center were Caitlin,

Hannah, and two grown-ups. Everyone else, including Hannah, looked like they were right at home. Caitlin was the only one who seemed to feel out of place.

I smiled at Caitlin and whispered, "That's how I sometimes feel at school. It's no big deal. Everyone here accepts you."

Caitlin looked surprised. I guess she had never thought about how anyone else feels except herself.

I lifted the camera and began to film the dancers swirling around and around the audience. Then one of the dancers suddenly jumped in front of Caitlin and pulled her onto the center of the floor. Other dancers grabbed people from the audience, too. The drummers got quiet.

I focused the camera on Caitlin. I thought it would be a good point in our report to talk about new cultural experiences and how they changed us and the way we think about things. Caitlin was certainly having a new cultural experience today!

One of the lead dancers took the mike.

"Now, these folks are going to dance a dance of jubilation with us."

Caitlin looked like she was going to run for the door at any second, but the woman who'd pulled her out of her seat had her by the arm.

"It's okay," the lead dancer said. "Everyone can dance the dance of jubilation. You're just going to do your own thing."

"But I'm not sure what to do," Caitlin told a dancer.

The woman said, "Just dance. What do you have to lose? We're all one here. You're among family. Come on now."

The dancers and audience members formed a circle. I kept filming.

When the drumming started again, everyone began to move any way they wanted. The lead dancer urged them to express what they felt in their hearts.

Caitlin tried to copy the steps some of the dancers were doing. Suddenly, she stumbled and tripped. Some of the dancers had to jump out of her way. Everyone looked puzzled. I think they thought she was doing a new dance!

Caitlin bumped into the table that held the food, and it crashed. She slid and fell in a puddle of bean dip. I couldn't believe what I was seeing through the video camera lens. I left the camera on the tripod and ran to the front of the room to help Caitlin.

As I reached for her hand, I slipped on the bean dip, too, and fell down next to Caitlin. We were both covered with the brown, sticky stuff. For a moment, we just looked at each other. At first, I thought Caitlin was going to cry. Her face crumpled and she covered her mouth.

I put my arm around her. "Are you hurt?"

Caitlin coughed, wiped her eyes, and burst out laughing.

"You should see yourself," she said. "You've got a bean on your nose."

I brushed my nose and smiled at her. "You look like you've been playing in the mud."

We started laughing and helped each other up. I grabbed a stack of napkins and gave some to Caitlin. We cleaned the bean dip off our hands and clothes.

"I'm so embarrassed," Caitlin said. "I wish I could hide somewhere."

"Don't worry about it," I said. "It was an accident."

Finally, the spilled food was mopped up and everyone settled down again. Everyone tried to convince Caitlin that it wasn't her fault. Anysa and Hannah took turns rubbing Caitlin's back, hugging her, and talking to her.

Finally, Daddy told Caitlin he had some good news for her.

"What is it?" Caitlin asked.

"Your father will be home in a few hours," Daddy said, smiling. "He wanted to surprise you, but I thought you needed to know now."

"Really?" Caitlin said. "That's great!" Her smile lit up the room.

Everyone hugged her and laughed. We all sat down and the program continued. Everyone had fun doing all the Kwanzaa activities. Caitlin and I filmed every event.

We were all pretty quiet on the ride back home. I

think everyone was tired after all the excitement. We dropped off Anysa and Hannah at Hannah's house. We all hugged good-bye. It took a lot for us all to become friends, but I could tell that Hannah and Caitlin liked each other now.

Chapter Twelve

The Surprise Ending

As soon as we got home, Caitlin called her father. I could hear her laughing and talking to him, but I couldn't hear what she was saying. She couldn't wait to pack her things and get home. I helped her put her clothes in her suitcase.

"Well, I think that's everything," I said. "If I find anything else, I'll bring it to you."

"Thanks. We can edit the video and write our report for school next week, if you want to," Caitlin said.

"Okay. Do you want to come over here?" I asked. I hoped she'd say yes.

"Sure, I'll come over," Caitlin said. "I really enjoyed spending the holidays with you."

"Yeah, I had a lot of fun," I said.

"Maybe you can spend next Christmas with us," Caitlin said.

"Maybe," I said. "We'll see. Momma is really strict about spending the holidays together. Maybe we can get together for Kwanzaa again, as long as we stay away from the bean dip."

Caitlin giggled. I picked up one of Caitlin's suitcases and followed her downstairs. She thanked Momma, Daddy, and Sandra, and hugged them all good-bye. Daddy grabbed her bags and put them in the van. Caitlin waved good-bye to us, and then she was gone.

A few days later, she called.

"Hi there!" Caitlin said. "I'm calling you on my new cell phone. My dad and mom bought it for me as a special Christmas gift. I can take pictures with it and I can use the Internet with it, too. It has six fun games you can play, and all kinds of cool features that I still have to learn and . . ."

I finally interrupted her. I can't stand it when she starts bragging.

"When are you coming over?" I asked.

"Oh, I'm on my way," Caitlin said. "I'm calling you from the car."

"Okay," I said. "See you soon."

When she got here, we worked for about an hour writing up our report. Then we started editing the video. For a while, everything went smoothly. We added subtitles, verbal descriptions, and music. It was coming along great, until we got to the Kwanzaa scene.

I had forgotten that Caitlin hadn't seen the entire video until now. She held her breath while she watched herself trip, fall, and knock over the food table.

"I, I didn't know you had all this on tape!" Caitlin said. "I would like to edit that out."

"Well, if we don't keep it in, we won't have enough film for a good presentation."

"Well, I don't want to show that part. Everyone will laugh at me," Caitlin said as she glared at me.

"Well, what are we going to do?"

Caitlin was quiet for a moment. "Maybe we could write a skit about Kwanzaa and present it to the class."

"That's a great idea!"

Caitlin and I worked all afternoon. Sometimes she got up to act out a part. Sometimes I acted out my ideas. We took turns typing it up on my computer.

"Maybe we can put it on at the next Kwanzaa gathering at the community center. It's the last day of Kwanzaa. It's called the *Karamu* feast."

"That's a great idea!" Caitlin said. She was quiet for a moment. "Do you think they'll let me come back?"

"Oh, they'll let you come," I said smiling. "But they'll think twice before they ask you to dance again!"

Caitlin laughed. She called her dad on her new cell phone to come and pick her up. When her father arrived, we hugged good-bye.

"Thanks for everything," Caitlin said. "I had fun. The skit is going to be great!"

"I'll call you and let you know when we'll pick you up for the Kwanzaa celebration."

"Great!" Caitlin said.

I went back upstairs to my room. I read our skit again. It was good! This was turning out to be a better idea than the video. I was glad Caitlin's clumsiness ruined the ceremony. I was sure we'd get an A+ for our skit. Besides, putting it on at the Kwanzaa ceremony would be a way to make up for all the confusion we caused the other day. I felt good about the way Caitlin and I had learned how to work together. We were finally friends.

I put the skit in a folder and got ready for bed. I slept better than I had in a long time.

The community center has their Kwanzaa *Karamu* feast on December 31. I knew from what I had read about Kwanzaa that that's usually when everyone exchanges handmade gifts. We'd already shared our gifts. I decorated purse-size mirrors with buttons for Momma and Sandra. I made Daddy a picture frame surrounded by buttons. Everyone seemed happy with their presents.

Momma gave me a gray sweater, just like I thought she would. I was surprised to discover that it was really pretty. Sandra gave me a photo album. Daddy gave all of us boxes of homemade chocolate candy. In my opinion, his gift was the best one of all.

"Daddy," I said, "can Caitlin and I put on a skit tonight?"

"Well, anyone can perform during the talent portion," Daddy said. "I'll put your name on the program."

"Thanks," I said. "Will you tape it for me?"

"Sure," Daddy said.

We picked up Caitlin and headed for the community center. We quietly practiced our lines. I felt pretty good about the skit we were going to put on, but I get nervous performing in front of a crowd. Caitlin seemed perfectly calm. She loves acting. I'd rather write or direct the play.

I waited anxiously until our names were called. Caitlin and I got up and began acting out the skit. I could really see a lot of myself in the main character. She didn't want to celebrate Kwanzaa, either. She did all kinds of funny things to get out of going to the Kwanzaa celebration. Caitlin's character tried to convince me that Kwanzaa was a wonderful celebration. She had all the funny lines, and she made everyone laugh with her comic expressions.

In the end, my character had to admit Kwanzaa was a wonderful celebration. Caitlin and I got a standing ovation! We took a bow and smiled at each other.

After the celebration, everyone came up to us to tell us how good our skit was. Daddy got the whole program on tape.

"That was funny," Sandra said.

"Thanks," I said. That's when I knew the skit was good. Sandra never says anything nice to me unless she really means it.

"I can't wait until Ms. Bailes see this," Caitlin said.

"She'll love it!" I said. "We're going to get an A+!"

Caitlin and I were so happy that we giggled all the way home.

Later that week, I started getting ready for the first day back at school.

"Hey, we're having a Johnson Girls-Back-to-School Celebration tonight," Daddy said. "Hurry up and come downstairs. We've got something for both of you."

No one can ever say that my parents aren't creative. They make up more fake holidays and celebrations than any family I've ever seen. What on earth is a Johnson Girls-Back-to-School Celebration?

Sandra and I went into the living room. Daddy had made popcorn. He said we'd watch old home videos to commemorate all the places we'd lived and how much we'd grown. This way, when we headed back to school tomorrow, we could be proud of how far we'd progressed. Sandra and I secretly rolled our eyes and made faces at each other. This sounded like it was going to be boring.

I watched myself on the video. It seemed as if I was always knocking something over, smashing into something, or kicking something by accident. Once I knocked down the Christmas tree. It was funny now. Everyone laughed, including me. But no one in my family was laughing on the video. They just picked me up, told me how cute I was, and put me down to knock over more things. Even Sandra was extra careful with me. I'd never noticed that before.

"I hope we've learned valuable lessons that can help us become better members of our family," said Daddy. "And remember, we are all one family. *Harambee! Harambee! Harambee! Harambee! Harambee! Harambee! Harambee!*"

We all shouted *"Harambee!"* with him. I have to admit that I had really enjoyed celebrating Kwanzaa. I would have enjoyed it even more if I hadn't spent so much time being mad because we had to celebrate it. I smiled when I remembered how I'd tried to get out of celebrating Hanukkah. Oh, well. Now I know how much fun celebrating a new holiday can be. I'd even made a new friend in Caitlin. I never thought that would happen!

I had just climbed into bed when Daddy came to

tuck me in. Now that I was older, he didn't always do that.

"Hey, pumpkin," he said, "I want you to know that I'm very proud of you and Caitlin. That's what this world needs, you know — more *Umoja*."

"Caitlin and I have plenty of unity now, after all we've been through during the holidays," I said.

"Well, everything that looks bad isn't, you know," Daddy said. He loves saying that. But I had to admit that he was right. Working on this project with Caitlin started out pretty bad. But now we're friends, and we have a great project to present at school.

"Good night!" Daddy said. "School starts tomorrow, and I want you up and ready to go, okay?"

"Okay, good night!"

I fell asleep thinking about everything Daddy had said.

I kept watching the clock at school, waiting for our turn to present our project. Caitlin squeezed my hand.

"Calm down," Caitlin whispered. "You'll do a great job!"

Ms. Bailes finally called our names. We went to the front of the room and told everyone about our project. I explained how Caitlin spent the holidays at our house. Caitlin told everyone that we had decided to film our Christmas and Kwanzaa celebrations. I switched on the video.

Everyone watched quietly. Caitlin sat up straight and seemed to hold her breath when the video got to the part where we put on our skit at the community center's Kwanzaa celebration. I had to admit that our skit was pretty funny. The whole class was laughing! Ms. Bailes laughed so hard she had to wipe her eyes.

I narrated the ending from my living room. Caitlin had never seen this part of the video. I stood in front of the Christmas tree and Daddy filmed it for me.

"This Christmas and Kwanzaa were very special to my partner, Caitlin, and me. We learned a lot about sharing, cooperation, and *Umoja*, which means unity. We also learned a lot about the meaning of friendship."

As THE END scrolled across the screen, I looked over at my partner, who was sitting up tall.

"Didn't we, partner?" I asked.

She beamed. "We sure did."

Everyone clapped for us.

"Girls," Ms. Bailes said, "may I see you both in the hall?"

I was shocked. I thought Ms. Bailes would like our project. She usually only told us to come into the hall when we were in trouble. I slowly followed Ms. Bailes and Caitlin into the hall. It seemed that no matter what I did, I couldn't win.

Ms. Bailes waited until the door was closed. Then she grabbed us and hugged us tightly. Caitlin and I exchanged surprised looks.

"I'm so proud of both of you!" Ms. Bailes whispered in our ears. "You girls have got yourselves an A+!"

I hugged Ms. Bailes and Caitlin, and smiled to myself. Theater camp, here I come!